Acting Out of Love

Sydney Campbell

Acting Out of Love

ISBN: 978-1-990231-14-8

Cover design by abu-chan
Editing by Megan Records

For SM, the original work husband.

Other books by Sydney Campbell:

Allie Styles Romance
Temptation (Book 1)
Deception (Book 2)
Reckonings (Book 3)
Beginnings (Book 4)

The Allie Styles Romance Boxed Set

Courtyard Tales of Contemporary Romance
Reawakening (Book 1)
Redemption (Book 2)
Reckless (Book 3)

Mountain Valley Romance
Acting out of Love (Book 1)
No Reservations Required (Book 2)
A Dash of Romance (Book 3)
Coming Around Again (Book 4)
Last Call (Book 5)
Roadside Attraction (Book 6)
At Close Range (Book 7)

CHAPTER ONE

Even though it was only 4:30 a.m. when I turned the key in the lock, I could tell it was going to be a beautiful day. Standing outside of my bakery, Franni's, I could see tulips in full bloom swaying in the breeze in the town square across the street. There wasn't a cloud in sight, and within hours the sun would be shining in the late May sky. I paused to admire the view, savouring the peaceful moments before my day began.

I walked inside and, as always, felt a twinge of nostalgia for my grandma. Shaking it off, I smiled as the bell jingled overhead. The shop had been hers and she'd willed it to me when she died three years earlier. I had the best memories of baking in the kitchen with her throughout my childhood and while I could have sold it, taking over seemed like the natural choice.

I flipped on the lights as I made my way through to the kitchen in the back. A large glass wall separated the kitchen from the front of the shop, allowing customers to watch us bake throughout the day. I turned on the ovens and pulled the breads and pastries out of the fridge and proofers. I hummed quietly to myself as I got into the routine, one I'd repeated every morning for the past three years.

Tess, one of my best friends and an employee, had asked to come in late that day. A big Hollywood movie had come rolling into our little town and she was dying to get a peek at the star, Mason Scott. She'd shown me pictures on her phone. Sure, he was cute, but I wasn't about to throw myself at the feet of some movie star. Just because he was famous didn't make him special. Or worth my time. But so little ever happened around here that I couldn't begrudge her for getting excited. What I hadn't counted on was Jax, my other best friend and employee, wanting to go with her. I was essentially on my own until nine a.m.

I spent the quiet hours baking the bread, rolls, and cinnamon buns I'd prepared the night before. Then I made brownies, cupcakes, and muffins. I had just stepped into the walk-in when I heard the bell jingle. I checked my watch, but it was only 6:40. The bakery wasn't open for another twenty minutes. I must've forgotten to lock the door behind me. I turned around, dusting my hands off on my apron and trying to shove a strand of hair from my face as I took my place behind the counter. I smiled at the customer, a stranger, which in and of itself was weird.

"Hi," I said. "We're not exactly open yet, but I can offer you a coffee."

The stranger looked up and flashed a smile, startling me for a moment with its brightness. He was probably in his early thirties, wearing a baseball hat pulled down low over his forehead. He had sunglasses on, so I couldn't see the colour of his eyes, but he had full lips and high cheekbones. A few stray curls poked out from beneath his hat.

"I was actually drawn by the smell of fresh cinnamon buns, but coffee sounds great," he said.

I turned to pour him a cup, grabbing some milk and sugar and handing the lot over to him. He took it from me and flashed that smile again.

"You don't look familiar," I said. "Kinda

strange for such a small town."

He laughed and took a sip of coffee.

"I'm here with the movie."

"Ah. I should've guessed. What do you do?"

He studied me for a moment and smiled again, but this time it was a small one, sly almost. He didn't say anything as he took another sip, but he never took his eyes off me. I blushed, which mortified me so much I blushed even harder. I turned my back to him, wiping down the back counter. He cleared his throat.

"I'm a grip," he said.

I turned back around.

"A grip? What's that?"

"I help set up everything for the camera, like tracks and crane shots."

"Oh. I guess that's the kind of stuff I never really think about. What goes on behind the camera and all that."

The oven timer went off and I smiled apologetically.

"I'm sorry. I've got to get that. Both my employees are off this morning. They went to check out your movie set, actually. Hoping to get a glimpse of Mason Scott."

"You didn't want to go along?" he asked.

I rolled my eyes.

"That kind of stuff doesn't interest me.

Sorry. No offense. I'm sure you work very hard, but I just never bought into the whole celebrity thing. I wouldn't know this Scott guy if I fell over him."

I walked back into the kitchen as he chuckled to himself and pulled the trays from the oven. Taking a basket down from the shelf overhead, I placed some of the cooled cinnamon buns in it and walked back out to the front.

"Can I offer you some buns?" I asked, blushing again as the words came out of my mouth. "Cinnamon, I mean. For your coffee. They're two-for-one before 9:00 a.m."

"That sounds great." He pulled out his wallet. "What do I owe you?"

I placed two buns into a paper bag and handed them to him.

"Three fifty, please."

He looked at me in shock, then looked around at the bakery, taking in all the products and empty shelves awaiting fresh-baked goods.

"Three fifty? How on earth do you pay rent here? I can't even buy a coffee for that much back home."

I shrugged.

"You're not home, are you?"

"No," he said, suddenly wistful. "I guess not."

He handed over a five-dollar bill and turned

to go, holding his coffee and bag in one hand and reaching for the door with the other.

"Have a nice day," I called.

Again with the dazzling smile.

"Thanks…"

"Katie."

"Thanks, Katie. I'm Mark."

I nodded and smiled as he walked out the door. I glanced up at the clock, saw it was almost seven, and got to work bringing out the rest of the pastries.

*

There was a line at the cash lane six people deep by the time Tess walked through the front door. I shot her a look and she scrambled into place behind the counter. She washed her hands, threw on an apron, and took over from me.

"Was it worth it?" I asked.

She shrugged.

"Well, I didn't get to see Mason Scott, but it was kind of neat watching them set up."

"You should've just come here. One of the. . .grips?. ..came in for coffee. He was cute enough."

I made my way back to the kitchen and got to work lining mini pie tins with a sugar crust.

Jax appeared and slid in beside me, working silently, occasionally tapping his foot.

"What's playing in your head?" I asked him.

He burst out laughing.

"*Hardest Button to Button.*"

"That explains the sporadic tapping. Can you get the lemon curd from the stove?" I asked.

Jax nodded and retrieved the pie filling. We spent the rest of the day finishing the tarts and decorating a cake for the upcoming Nelson wedding. We chatted on and off, but my mind kept drifting back to my morning visitor.

He was *cute.*

CHAPTER TWO

When my alarm went off at 3:30 a.m., I wanted to cry. Normally, I didn't mind getting up at that hour. I was used to it. But the night before, I'd foolishly let Tess talk me into going out for dinner. She was applying for an MBA program and wanted to go over her application. At least that's what she told me. But between dessert and drinks, I didn't get home until almost nine, which meant I'd be working the entire day on less than 6 hours sleep.

I groaned and pushed back the covers. Rolling out of bed, I resigned myself to the fact that it would be a horrible day, but at the end of it I'd climb right back into bed and have a blissful night's sleep. After stumbling through a shower and a cup of coffee, I grabbed my keys and headed to the bakery.

It must have been about 6:00 a.m. when I heard the tap on the door. I looked up through the glass partition and saw Mark standing outside, baseball cap firmly in place. I made my way towards him, pausing to turn on the coffee machine, and unbolted the lock. I opened the door a crack and smiled.

"Still another hour until we open," I said.

"I know, but they get really mad when I'm not on set at seven, and I knew you'd be here. Any chance I could get a few more cinnamon buns?"

I opened the door and stood aside. He touched the brim of his cap as he passed me, making his way into the store. I went back behind the counter and picked up a pair of tongs.

"How many?" I asked. "If you can wait a few minutes, I'm brewing some fresh coffee."

"A dozen please, and yes on the coffee."

He watched me pack the buns into a box and then wandered around the shop, looking through the glass at all our creations. I stood back and said nothing, letting him explore. When he finally returned to the counter, I handed him the box. He took it from me but placed it down on the counter.

"They taste just like my grandmother's," he said. "I couldn't believe it when I took that first bite. It was something I hadn't experienced in 15 years."

I stopped what I was doing and studied him. He wasn't bullshitting me. I could tell by the faraway gaze in his eyes. And since he was a grip and not an actor, I knew he was actually remembering. The corner of his mouth pulled up a little when he noticed me staring at him. He self-consciously pulled his hat down lower and cleared his throat.

"How about that coffee?" he asked.

Startled, I stood up straight and turned to look at the coffee maker. Sure enough, the pot was ready. I poured him a cup and mixed in two milks, two sugars—just like I'd seen him do the day before. I handed it to him as he handed me a twenty. I gave him his change, our fingers lightly touching as he took the bills from my hand.

"I don't suppose you'd share the recipe, would you?" he asked, almost shyly.

I thought about it for a moment.

"I'll tell you what. If you're willing to get here at the butt-crack of dawn, I'll show you how to make them."

His eyes lit up. Without the sunglasses, I could see they were a clear blue. I couldn't help but smile in response.

"What time?"

"Four-thirty. I usually make them the night before, so if I'm doing them in the morning, they'll need time to rise."

"Don't say another word. I'll be here."

He took his box from the counter and walked out the front door.

*

When Tess came in later that morning, she zeroed in on my good mood like a rat to fresh garbage.

"Why are you so chipper?" she asked suspiciously.

"What do you mean? Can't I be in a good mood?"

She cocked her head.

"With the customers, sure. But with us?"

I said nothing and kept putting loaves of bread on the shelves while Tess arranged cupcakes in the display fridge.

"You can't fool me. There's something going on with you. Wait a minute. Did that guy come back this morning?"

I bit my lip, trying not to smile, but it was no use. Tess had always been able to see right through me. It was like some kind of superpower. She was tiny—barely 5′ tall and maybe 110 pounds–and that one ability made her my biggest threat. I could never get any bullshit past her.

"Yes. He came back."

"Oh my god. You have to take me to set and introduce me. Maybe he knows Mason Scott. What am I saying? Of course, he knows Mason Scott! Please! Katie, please!"

"Forget it, Tess. I don't even know the guy's last name. I'm not going to a movie set like some crazy fan. I'm not planning to see him again, either."

I turned my back as I said that last part, knowing if she'd seen my eyes she'd know I was lying.

"Why wouldn't you see him again?"

"Because he's only in town for a couple of weeks. I have no interest in a casual relationship. You know that."

"And you know Jax is gay, right? Because he's the only man I ever see you spend time with. I'm not sure where you plan to meet anyone else since you spend all your time here."

"Can we just drop this?"

The oven timer went off and I smiled triumphantly. Turning on my heel, I hightailed it to the kitchen to pull the trays from the oven.

The bell jingled as the first customers of the day walked in. I left the kitchen, knowing Jax would be back from the market at any moment, and rejoined Tess to greet the crowds.

*

Jax and I were cleaning the kitchen at the end of the day when the phone rang. I kept wiping down the counters as he took the call and I could tell it was a catering job. Judging from the time he spent writing, I figured it was a big one. He hung up and walked back over to the racks, laying fresh sheets of parchment down on the empty trays.

"You going to tell me who that was?" I asked.

He turned and grinned.

"Party this weekend. Fifty guests. Full luncheon: apps, sit-down meal, sweet table."

"Oh good lord. Are we going to be able to squeeze in the prep or do I need to bring someone in off-hours?"

"We'll be fine. Maybe you can get a few more trays in tomorrow morning so it'll free up the afternoon for me?"

I nodded, agreeing it was a good plan. Plus, I knew I'd have a helper. Or at least I hoped I would. There was still a good chance Mark wouldn't even show up. He certainly didn't owe me anything.

CHAPTER THREE

I got to the bakery the next morning and a small flurry of butterflies erupted in my belly as I saw Mark standing there, holding two cups of coffee. The ever-present baseball cap was pulled low and he wore a light jacket to protect against the cool breeze. He was staring across the street into the square at the same patch of tulips I'd been admiring the day before. He had a faraway look in his eyes and I paused, not wanting to get any closer for fear of disturbing the moment. I was happy to take the time to study him.

He was a good half-foot taller than me. I wasn't short, but at 5'4" I wasn't particularly tall. He was at least six feet. His curly hair was still hidden by the cap, but now that I'd seen those blue eyes I could see them in my sleep. In fact, I had. Every last detail of them. I smoothed my jacket down over my stomach before approaching. He started at the noise, then smiled and raised a coffee-laden hand in greeting. His hands were so big. I could just imagine what it would feel like to have one of my own wrapped in them. I shook my head. *Stop it.*

"Hey," I said. "I'm impressed you got up this early."

"I figured it would take a while to make the coffee, so I brought some from the hotel."

I took one of the cups from him and mumbled my thanks. Then I turned and unlocked the door. I flipped on the lights as we walked in and he put down his cup to strip off his jacket. He was wearing a black T-shirt and jeans, and the muscles in his upper arms made me weak in the knees. I cleared my throat and headed into the back to switch on the ovens.

"Can you get the coffee machine?" I called.

"Sure thing."

I grabbed an apron from the wall and continued to the bathroom. I shut the door and leaned back against it, trying the calm myself. He was a man. I was a woman. That was all.

Fine, so he was an attractive man. And we were there, alone in the bakery at 4:30 in the morning, but it didn't mean anything. He wanted to make cinnamon buns. That was it.

I looked at myself in the mirror. My dirty blond hair fell just to my shoulders, straight no matter what I did to it. My hazel eyes stared back at me, unsure whether they wanted to be green or brown that day. I had a small smattering of freckles that refused to go away no matter how old I got. I picked up a hair tie from the shelf below the mirror and pulled my hair up into a ponytail. Then I grabbed a bandanna and tied it around my hair—my preferred method over the hairnet. At the last moment, I dug around through the basket on the shelf and unearthed a lipstick. Shaking my head, I pulled off the cap and applied the muted red shade.

By the time I walked back into the kitchen, Mark was ready, apron on, and awaiting instruction. He was just looking at me, eyebrows raised in expectation.

"I'm in your hands," he said. "Tell me what to do."

It took me a moment to get my bearings, but I told him to grab the flour and start measuring it out while I gathered the other ingredients. I took my place beside him at the long counter and showed him how to mix everything before letting the machine do the heavy work of kneading. We worked together in silence for a bit, me occasionally giving instructions. He was clumsy, clearly never having been in a kitchen before, but god help me I found it charming. Especially when he glanced over at me with that smidge of flour between his eyebrows. I couldn't help myself. I reached out and brushed it away. He caught my wrist and held it there for a moment as we locked eyes.

"Hey," he said.

"Hey," I said, not moving a muscle.

Neither of us broke eye contact. My breathing deepened as that swarm of butterflies was set loose once again. Slowly, so slowly I thought I was imagining it, he leaned in towards me. I couldn't believe what was about to happen, but I didn't budge. As I closed my eyes, I felt his lips brush against mine. I let go of the breath I didn't realize I'd been holding and let him kiss me. It was...exquisite. Maybe West Coast men knew something about kissing that I'd been missing out on because within seconds my head was swimming.

He let go of my wrist and I felt his hand on the back of my head, insistent. I opened my eyes to find him gazing at me and it was only then I understood I hadn't kissed him back. I parted my lips slightly and felt the tip of his tongue swipe my bottom lip. I put down my rolling pin and wound my arms around his neck. Needing no further encouragement, he wrapped his other arm around my waist and pulled me in.

I don't know how long we were there. How long can one go without breathing? But oxygen was a secondary concern. Mark was my only priority. Not breaking that kiss was my mission.

Eventually, he drew away, a shy smile on his face. It was nothing like the dazzler he usually flashed. He reached up to run his hand through his hair and started as he touched the baseball cap. A look of mild frustration passed across his face I didn't understand, but honestly, my mind was still on the kiss.

"I'm sorry," he said. "I didn't mean for that to happen."

But he didn't let go.

"Don't apologize. I enjoyed it immensely."

He grinned. I got up on my tiptoes and kissed him lightly on the mouth to show him I meant it. He groaned softly. The oven buzzer went off. I gently released his hand from my waist and stepped back.

"Ovens are preheated. We should roll out the buns and get them in to bake. You ready?"

Mark gave me a quick salute and straightened out his apron.

"Teach me."

The mood was much lighter—and easier—between us after that kiss. I laughed at his ineptitude with the rolling pin and his complete inability to make icing. He loved playing with the brown sugar and cinnamon, though. When I left him to proof some rolls, I returned to find him creating a small beach scene on the counter. I burst into laughter.

"Did you never bake as a child?" I asked.

He shook his head.

"Nope. Never set foot in the kitchen. My mom passed away when I was young and my grandmother moved in to help my dad raise me and my siblings. The kitchen was her domain, and I was not allowed in."

"Wow. I'm so sorry about your mom. What a loss that was at such a young age. How many siblings do you have?"

Mark stared at me for a full thirty seconds before shifting his gaze away. He gave a small laugh of disbelief before answering me.

"Five. I have five siblings."

"Do they all work in the film business?"

"No." He laughed. "We all had very different aspirations for when we got older. But enough about me. Tell me about you. I'm guessing you've lived here your whole life?"

"I have, aside from college. Here, watch, we need to pack the buns onto the tray like this. They're going to grow together as they bake. I've traveled a little, but not enough."

"Where have you been?"

"Washington. New York. London—but it was a very short school trip. Mexico for a couple of girls' trips. What about you? Do you travel? Oh. I guess you do."

He laughed.

"What about family? Big? Small?"

"Small. I'm an only child. My mom passed away last year. My dad is in his late seventies. I was a late-in-life baby for them. They thought my dad was sterile because he'd had the mumps. Turns out that wasn't the case."

"I'm sorry about your mom."

I took a breath and tried to keep it together. The memory was still so fresh I cried every time I thought about her. But I didn't want to cry in front of Mark.

"How did you end up with a bakery?" he asked, tactfully changing the subject.

"Well, your grandmother made cinnamon buns, my grandmother owned a bakery. She willed it to me, and when she passed away, I couldn't bring myself to sell it. Instead, I've devoted the last few years to trying to make it work. I love baking and it makes me feel closer to her."

"That's amazing. Finding true happiness right in your own backyard. I'm jealous."

I stopped midway to the oven, tray in hand, turning that thought over in my head.

"It's funny. I spend so much of my time wishing for more, I never even looked at it like that."

I slid the tray into the oven and closed the door. When I turned around, he was right there.

"It's special," he said. "Trust me. I have traveled the world and I've never found anything like you've got here. What more could you want?"

I looked down, suddenly shy again.

"I like baking cakes. I want to make cakes. High-end catering kind of thing. It's been kind of impossible to get off the ground, but I've been working on a plan to clear the way for myself." I paused and glanced up at him. "Are you not happy with what you do?"

He considered that for a moment.

"I always wanted to be…in the film business. I just never really considered the consequences. The loneliness. I move around a lot. I don't get to form attachments." He laughed softly. "It's what makes meeting people like you so difficult. Knowing that in a few weeks, I'll be packing my bags and waiting for my next contract."

The reality of that statement slammed home. I slid out from between him and the oven and got busy prepping the day's goods. He watched me silently for a while and then got to work washing dishes.

"I didn't mean I do *this* all the time, you know. In fact, I've never done this."

I laughed.

"What? Baking? We already established that."

He walked up to me and put his hands on my shoulders.

"I'm serious. I don't make it a habit of kissing strange women. I like you. We had a moment there. I'd have been a fool not to act on it."

"You're very suave. You should be a movie star."

I turned and entered the walk-in fridge. He followed, laughing. I turned and he kissed me. It was meant to be quick, I could tell, but he changed his mind at some point and I was powerless to resist. The cold temperature of the fridge was no match for the heat between us. I'd be lying if I said I'd never fantasized about sex in the walk-in—anyone who's worked in a kitchen has—but I'd never imagined it might actually happen.

Just then, I heard the bell over the door.

"Katie?" Tess called out.

"Shit!" I said, pulling back.

"Shit!" Mark said, checking the time. "Oh crap. It's almost six-thirty. I've got to go."

I looked at him, then out towards the front of the shop.

"There's a back door," I said, hesitating. I didn't want him thinking I was ashamed, but nor did I need questions from Tess.

"Perfect," he said.

I moved past him to greet Tess out front, providing enough distraction for Mark to slip out the back. Once I got her up to speed on what needed to be done, I returned to the kitchen to catch my breath. I saw a note scribbled on the order pad by the phone and quickly walked over. *Thanks for the lesson. Hope to see you soon.*

I ripped the page off the pad, folded it up, and put it in my apron pocket, smiling as I did.

CHAPTER FOUR

The next couple of days were crazy busy. With the warmer weather came the tourists, and with the cast and crew from the film shoot, our small-town population was exploding. It was fine with me—more people equaled more coffee and pastries. But we also had the added pressure of the upcoming party that weekend, so Jax and I were working overtime to get that menu ready.

Still, with everything going on, it didn't escape my notice that Mark hadn't come back. Two mornings in a row I'd worked, anticipating his tap on the door, but it never came. I knew he was busy. Tess kept me up-to-date with constant reports on the shoot. They still had two weeks left here, and she was intent on meeting Mason Scott. Or at least catching a glimpse of him.

On the third day, Tess blocked my way as I was returning to the kitchen after the morning rush. I looked at her, startled.

"What's up?"

"You tell me," she said.

"I have no idea what you're talking about."

Tess just threw up her hands and rolled her eyes.

"Come on, Katie. You've been distracted, starry-eyed, and generally not yourself. What the hell is up?"

I said nothing. Tess just stared.

"You're still seeing him."

I let out a sigh.

"How do you do that?"

"It's a gift. So what's the problem? How come I haven't even met him yet?"

"I don't know. He was here a few days ago, and then I never saw him again. But he left me this." I pulled out the note and handed it to Tess, who read it and smiled.

"We can fix this," she said.

"Tess—"

"No, I'm serious. It's easy. What did you say he does?"

"He's a grip."

"Right. After lunch, we'll box up a few dozen cupcakes and bring them over to set."

"Tess! This has nothing to do with me. You're just using me to get on set."

"Not true. Fine, we both win, but I see that as an advantage." She stared at me with pleading eyes. "Katie. I just want a peek."

"Why? What's so special about him? He's just a person."

"He's Mason Scott! And he's in my town."

"You care far too much about these things."

"So? After lunch?"

I stepped around her and walked into the kitchen, leaving her to the customers. Without turning, I called back to her.

"Fine. You box the cupcakes."

*

After the lunch crowd filtered out, Tess and I grabbed our stuff and left Jax to mind the shop. He was pretty pissed he couldn't come, but someone had to stay behind. Tess carried a few boxes of cupcakes with a paper bag resting on top.

"What's in the bag?" I asked.

"Trust me."

We walked to the set, which was about fifteen minutes away. It was a gorgeous day. It felt like the whole town was out enjoying the weather, rather than being stuck inside at work. There was a mix of familiar and unfamiliar faces in the street, but we smiled at everyone. Tess chattered on and on about the production. She'd been reading item after item online and couldn't believe she'd finally figured out a way to worm her way past security.

At the moment, she was talking about some dress. Apparently, the lead actress, Jessica Thompson, was getting married during filming. Their next location was Switzerland and she and her fiancé decided to tie the knot in the Alps. Tess had been talking about it for weeks.

After a while, I just tuned out, having zero interest in anything to do with celebrities. Their lives confused me. I couldn't understand wanting to live in the public eye like that. I was a much more private person. Just the thought of that life made me shudder.

We turned the corner off Main Street onto Palmer Avenue and up ahead I could see the cranes set up with the bright lights. There were trailers everywhere and I couldn't imagine where they all came from. Sure, we had RV rental places in town, but these were huge and fancy, with sides that popped out. As we got nearer, I approached a tall, thin man with a headset and a walkie-talkie tucked into his belt.

"Excuse me—" I started, but was quickly silenced by Tess, who shoved her elbow into my side. She stepped in front of me.

"Hi. We're here to deliver cupcakes," she said, full of confidence.

The guy eyed her skeptically and reached for his walkie-talkie. Tess quickly handed me the boxes and grabbed the bag. She thrust it at the guy.

"Here. I brought you a little something special. A couple of cupcakes, and a couple of special brownies, if you know what I mean."

A slow smile spread across his face. He knew exactly what she meant. I filed it away for later that Tess had been making pot brownies in my kitchen, but at that moment I was just impressed it had worked. He pointed towards our destination and we walked right in.

"Do you see him?" Tess whispered.

I shook my head, looking at all the crew members. They swarmed down on us as we delivered the boxes to the woman standing behind the craft services table. There were large umbrellas set up to shield them from the sun, which at this point in the afternoon was beating down without mercy. It was a good thing there were so many people because there was no way the icing would have survived the heat.

"Quiet on set!" a voice called.

Everyone stilled and people quietly crept away and resumed their positions. Tess squeezed my arm.

"Oh my god, oh my god, they're going to shoot. I'm going to see him!"

"I don't see Mark anywhere, though. We should go."

"ARE YOU CRAZY?"

"Shhh!" hissed the woman behind the table.

Tess cringed in apology and turned her attention to the set, where a tall, beautiful woman was having her hair touched up.

"Holy shit. That's Jessica Thompson. Oh my god. She's beautiful."

"Shut up, Tess."

I stood there watching, mesmerized despite myself. She was beautiful. Unearthly, almost. I was so distracted by her that I didn't even notice when Mark stepped onto the set. It was only when the director screamed "Action" that I started and noticed him standing beside Jessica.

"There he is," I whispered to Tess, pointing.

"There who is?" she asked.

"Mark. Right there."

She followed my finger, gripping my arm so

tightly I almost fainted.

"YOU'RE SECRETLY DATING MASON SCOTT?" she screamed.

"I never said dating," I offered meekly, as the director yelled "CUT" and all eyes turned to us.

I was mortified. But I was also shocked and rooted to the spot. My brain understood what Tess was frantically babbling on about in my ear, but I couldn't reconcile Mark and Mason being the same person. I had no time to think about it, though, as a very large man with very large forearms was walking towards us quickly, giving us the universal signal for "Get the fuck out."

"Shit," Tess muttered. She grabbed my arm and steered me towards the exit. I was practically running when I heard Mark—or Mason—calling from behind me.

"Katie! Wait!"

"Mason!" the director screamed. "Take your place. First positions, everyone. We're going again right now."

CHAPTER FIVE

We walked at a brisk pace back to the bakery, Tess going on and on about how she couldn't believe I didn't know it was Mason Scott while I was just trying to clear my head. I couldn't understand why he'd lied to me. He'd had plenty of opportunities to tell the truth. And it wasn't even a lie of omission. He'd given me a fake name and job description. My confusion morphed into anger and by the time we reached the bakery I was in a rage.

"Katie."

"What?" I roared, turning on Tess. She shrank back.

"Sorry."

"No," I said, shaking my head. "I'm sorry. I

know you want answers. I don't have any."

"Did you kiss him?"

I sighed.

"I did."

"OH MY GOD!" she squealed, clamping her hand over her mouth. "I'm sorry. I can't help it. You kissed him."

"Yes. I kissed him. But he lied to me. I'm furious, Tess."

"What? Why? You're dating a movie star!"

"That doesn't give him carte blanche to toy with me. God, he must have been laughing at me. *I wouldn't know Mason Scott if I fell over him.* Dammit. Come on, let's get back to work."

I pushed open the door and made my way inside. The shop was empty and the shelves mostly bare. Jax looked up from his phone and caught my expression.

"Didn't go as planned?" he asked.

"I'll say," I laughed bitterly.

Tess couldn't contain herself.

"Katie's dating Mason Scott!"

Jax dropped his phone on the counter and leapt up from his stool.

"WHAT?"

The two of them starting chattering like old ladies at a tea party while I went to the back to wash up and put my apron back on. I was still in mild shock, but the rage had simmered

36

down a little. I was still furious, but there were things to do and I didn't have the time to waste one more second on Mason Scott.

*

Unfortunately, the choice wasn't mine alone. Within minutes, Jax was following me around, hounding me with questions.

"Mason Scott was here?"

"Yes."

"WHEN?"

"He was here a few times. In the early morning. We made cinnamon buns together."

"TESS! They made cinnamon buns together! In my kitchen!" Jax was beside himself.

I stopped what I was doing and faced him.

"Jax. This is not a big deal, and it won't be happening again. I had no idea who he was. I have no interest in dating a movie star."

Jax grabbed hold of the counter and feigned passing out. Tess appeared by his side and the two of them just stood there, incredulous looks on their faces.

"Whyever not?" Tess asked.

"You've known me long enough to answer that question yourself," I said.

"Please. This is not about you finding love or some lifelong relationship. This is about you having fun. Why can't you just have fun?"

"I'm not interested."

Jax pushed Tess aside and took me by the shoulders.

"Listen to me," he said. "You know every man in this town. I have no idea who you think you're going to meet in the next few weeks. What I do know is that in two weeks, Mason Scott will be leaving and you'll have lost your chance to experience something truly unique."

I said nothing. He took it as a sign to continue.

"I'm not saying I condone throwing oneself at a celebrity for the sake of it. But you two met and formed an honest connection. Don't let the fact that he's one of the most famous people in the world stop you from getting to know him."

That was it. I gently removed his hands from my shoulders and stepped away. I grabbed a few plastic bags and started bagging bread products for the next day's day-old basket.

"Forget it. Subject closed."

From the corner of my eye, I saw them exchange glances. *Screw it.* I carried on with my work.

*

It was six o'clock and Jax and I were cleaning

the kitchen while Tess swept the front. Jax was telling me about some band he was going out to see that night with some friends. I was thinking it had been a long time since I'd gone out to hear live music.

"Anything I'd like?" I asked him.

"I think so. They're kinda folky, with a classic rock sound. But with kind of an edge, if you know what I mean," Jax draped his dish towel over the rack and peeled off his apron. "But I thought you didn't go out on work nights."

"I don't. But it's nice to dream."

Jax laughed as I took off my own apron and hung it on the hook. I glanced up to check Tess's progress. Through the glass, I saw her standing stock-still, staring out the front window towards the town square.

"What's up, Tess?" I called.

She slowly turned towards us, wearing an awed expression.

"I think Mason Scott is waiting for you across the street."

"What?" I said.

I slowly made my way to the front of the store. Jax did not have my hesitation. He raced past me, screeching to a halt as he got to the front window.

"Oh my god, oh my god, oh my god." He

was running his hand through his hair, turning in circles.

I looked out and sure enough, there he was. Baseball cap, sunglasses, faded jeans. The townspeople were just walking by, leaving him be. I was sure most of them recognized him, but that's just the kind of community we were. Oh sure, we'd talk about him nonstop amongst ourselves, but we'd never stoop so low as to harass him in public.

I contemplated the back door but quickly realized I was being childish. There was no reason for me not to go out there. Of course, the moment I crossed that street the gossip in town would spread like wildfire. I was the town good girl. If I hadn't accumulated enough social credit by this point to withstand a little chatter, I never would.

I drew myself up and tucked in the front of my T-shirt.

Then I smoothed down my hair and wiped the sweat off the palms of my hands.

"You're going out there?" Tess asked.

"I am."

She gave me a pat on the back and a huge smile.

"Remember what I said." Jax gave me a meaningful look. I nodded, opened the door and crossed the street.

CHAPTER SIX

A slow, tentative smile spread across Mason's face as I walked towards him. I couldn't help but see him in a new light and I marveled at how stupid I'd been. The baseball hat, the glasses, the impossible good looks—of course, he was a movie star. My heart still skipped a beat, despite my anger.

"Hey," he said. "Thanks for coming out."

I didn't say a word.

"You're angry," he said.

"You lied to me."

"I know. I'm so sorry."

"Why did you lie to me?"

He sighed and looked out over the square, the light golden in those last hours before sunset. Then he took off his sunglasses and turned to me. *Those eyes.*

"Do you know how long it's been since I met someone who didn't know who I was? Since I've gotten to spend time with someone who wasn't either paid to or wanted something from me? Who saw *me*, the person, instead of the movie star? When we met, I couldn't believe you didn't know who I was. At first, I thought you were kidding, but when I came back the next day…Katie. It was a chance I couldn't pass up. To have a normal conversation with someone. To do normal things."

I swallowed. Hard. That was not the answer I'd expected and I wasn't sure how to respond. When I thought about it from his perspective, it did make sense. But the fact remained that he lied to me. I couldn't get past that.

"I was going to tell you, I swear. That's why I hadn't been by in a couple of days. I was trying to figure out how. And then you showed up, and god, that was not how I wanted it to happen. Please. Give me another chance."

I pointed to a bench up ahead, right by the gazebo.

"Let's go sit down," I said.

He nodded eagerly and walked with me.

"I hear what you're saying," I said. "But

what was your plan? I mean, I looked like a complete idiot today."

"You didn't. I'm sorry. I'm the one who looked like an ass. God, Jessica gave me such shit when I told her what was going on. I promise—no one thinks anything of the sort."

"And your plan?"

"Well, I was going to tell you who I was and hope you still wanted to be friends anyway."

"I live a very private life, Mason."

"I get that, Katie. I'm only in town for a couple more weeks. We get along. I really like you. Just give me a shot."

"Give you a shot?"

He shifted uncomfortably.

"Look, I'm not asking for anything romantic here. I get that I fucked that up. But like I said, I like you. As a person. You're fun to be with. You're passionate and interesting and it's so refreshing to just *be* with you."

I thought about it for a moment. It was only a couple of weeks. There was zero pressure. Why should I pass this up? Even though I didn't care who he was, I still liked him. And knowing he had an expiry date meant I wouldn't be tempted to get romantically involved.

"What are you doing for dinner?" I asked.

He sat up, startled.

"Well, actually—"

"No, it's fine," I interrupted. "Who am I to think a big movie star doesn't have plans for dinner?"

With that, Mason pulled out his phone and sent off a quick text. A moment later he got a response, nodded, and put the phone away.

"I have no plans for dinner," he said.

I tilted my head and laughed nervously.

"What did you do?"

"Nothing you have to worry about. Where do you want to go?"

"I was going to cook tonight. Korean beef over rice. Interested?"

As soon as the words were out of my mouth, I felt ridiculous. Sure, maybe Mark would've come over for dinner. But did I really ask Mason Scott to come over for stir-fry? Yes, he'd told me he was the same person, but I was already beginning to see that wasn't true.

"That sounds amazing. I haven't had a home-cooked meal in months."

"Oh," I said, surprised. "That hadn't even occurred to me. I guess room service and restaurants get tiresome after a while?"

"They really do. Let's go. Lead the way."

*

44

I took him on the scenic route back to my apartment, taking in all the eyes that carefully averted when we walked past. I wasn't the only one.

"You're all very polite here," Mason remarked.

"We're classy like that," I grinned. "Don't worry. They'll all be talking over dinner tonight."

He laughed knowingly.

"Where did you grow up?" I asked.

"L.A.," he said. "Big city boy from day one."

"Well, small towns are something special. I mean, I'm sure people are the same everywhere, but there's a vibe in small towns you don't get anywhere else."

"I like small towns. It's always been my dream to buy some property in a place like this and have somewhere to retreat to when I'm ready to block out the rest of the world."

"Why haven't you?"

"Never found just the right place."

We stopped in front of my building and I pointed.

"This is me. Not what you're used to, but I call it home, so be kind."

Mason took my hand to prevent me from walking through the front door. I turned to him.

"Stop it," he said. "It's just me, okay? Don't start getting weird."

I nodded. He was right. If this was going to work, for either of us, that was how it had to be.

"Well, then," I said. "Let's go have dinner."

CHAPTER SEVEN

My apartment was a small one-bedroom. I had a separate kitchen and living room, but no real dining room. There was space in the kitchen for a small table, and I usually ate either there or on the couch. Just by luck, I'd picked up some tulips the day before and they were in a vase on the hallway table, so at least it looked kind of homey. I picked up a few tossed items of clothing as I made my way through the apartment, Mason close behind.

"I like it," he said.

"Thanks. It's small, but it's perfect for me."

I threw my collection of laundry into the coat closet and flashed him a quick smile. He laughed and followed me into the kitchen. As I pulled out my prepped ingredients from the fridge, he looked around at all my baking accessories. There were a lot. I may have blushed.

"Job hazard," I said.

"I can imagine. I don't even know what half these things are for. What's this?" he asked, holding up a small metal tube.

"To make the shells for cannoli."

He practically drooled.

"Will you teach me?"

"Not tonight," I laughed. "Go sit in the living room. This won't take long. Everything is ready to go. Another job hazard."

He wandered out of the kitchen into the living room and slowly perused my bookshelves. I watched him through the corner of my eye, his finger trailing along the spines, stopping every once in a while to pull out a volume.

"You have a lot of books," he called.

"I like to read."

"I just meant that so many people read on an e-reader these days. It's nice to be able to see what you're into. I miss turntables and CD players for that reason. No one ever has their musical tastes on display anymore."

I paused as I swirled the oil around in the wok.

"That's true. I never really thought about it before."

"I see you like Jonathan Tropper. I love his stuff. I'd love to star in an adaptation of one of his books. Did you see *This is Where I Leave You?*"

"I did. I loved that movie."

"I haven't read all of these. Are they all good?"

"They all contain the exact same elements—a baby, a death, an infidelity—but each one is unique and amazing."

He nodded and flipped through a few pages.

"Take it," I said.

He looked over at me through the open doorway and smiled.

"Thanks. I'll get it back to you."

I steamed the rice while I stir-fried the beef, and by the time Mason was done snooping through all my stuff, dinner was on the table. He came in to join me, grabbing the vase of flowers from the hall and depositing it right between our dinner plates.

I sat down to join him, handing him a glass of wine.

"This is just so…nice. Thank you. Very out of the ordinary for me."

"I'm eating with Mason Scott at my kitchen table. I'd say we're far from ordinary."

He raised his eyebrow and I rolled my eyes. I lifted my glass.

"To new friends," I said.

He clinked my glass with his.

"To new friends."

*

After dinner, we moved to the living room and settled on the couch to polish off the bottle of wine. We talked and laughed for hours, and by the time I checked my watch, I was shocked to see it was nine o'clock. He caught my expression and pulled out his phone.

"I'm sorry. You've been up forever. You must be exhausted. I should go."

I opened my mouth to protest, but a big yawn escaped instead and I realized he was probably right.

"When do you have to be on set tomorrow?" I asked.

"I don't. We're turning over into nights, so I have a couple of days off. You? What hours do you work?"

"Normally 4:30 to noon, but we're handling a big party this weekend so I've been putting in double shifts."

"Holy shit. Katie. That's nuts. Go to bed."

"Do you want me to call you a cab? I

imagine you're staying at The Elway?"

"I am, and no, thank you."

"Are you sure?"

"Positive. I, uh, have a driver."

He looked so sheepish I laughed.

"Of course you do.

*

When Jax and Tess showed up at work the next morning, the questions were flying. The last they knew I was crossing the street to give him crap. When I told them it had ended with dinner in my apartment, I thought their heads would explode.

"Did you sleep with him?" Jax demanded.

"NO! We're just friends."

"Just friends," Tess snorted. "Right."

"It's true."

"Why on earth would you do that?" Jax asked.

"Haven't we had this conversation already?"

Tess sighed, looking dejected.

"You're telling me there's no possibility of casual sex here?"

"None."

They both looked disappointed in me.

Jax jumped down from the stool he'd been perched on and headed for the kitchen.

"Well, I for one have a ton of work to get done if we're going to be ready for this party tomorrow. Doors open in five, ladies. And Katie, this is not over."

CHAPTER EIGHT

It was a busy Friday, but despite the fact I spent most of the afternoon in front with Tess, Jax still managed to get the rest of the baking done for the party. It wasn't a huge guest list, but it was an important one. Fifty of the most influential people in town, the crowd responsible for throwing every fundraiser that would take place over the next year. If they were happy with the food, we'd be set.

It was close to six when I rang the last customer out. The shelves were bare and there were maybe half a dozen pastries left in the case. Jax came out front, untying his apron.

"Wow. That was a day," he said.

"Tomorrow will be a day," Tess said,

counting out the last of the bills from the cash drawer.

"But then Sunday I'm off. . ." I smiled wickedly. I did feel bad leaving the two of them alone on our busiest day, but I hadn't had time off in over three weeks. I was burnt out and looking forward to a day of doing absolutely nothing.

"Why don't you go? We'll close up," Jax said, gesturing vaguely around the store.

"You sure? I'm wiped," I said.

"Go. Rest. I'll see you in the morning and help you get set up before joining Tess here."

"Perfect. See you then."

I went in back, washed up, grabbed my bag, and left the bakery for the day.

*

It was a gorgeous night and as I rounded the corner off Main Street, I almost bumped right into Mason. He gave me a sheepish grin which told me he'd been waiting for me.

"You could've come in, you know," I said.

"I know. Figured I'd surprise you. I know you're tired and have a big day tomorrow. I just wanted to walk you home."

"That would be lovely," I said, falling into step beside him. "What did you do today?"

"Honestly? I mostly slept."

"Jealous."

He laughed.

"I can imagine. You have any time off coming up?"

"I'm off Sunday. I can't wait."

"Big plans?"

"Absolutely none. I'm going to stay home and do nothing. Maybe Netflix. Maybe wine. Definitely pajamas."

"So I can't coax you into giving me a tour of your charming town?"

"Don't you have work?"

"I told you. We're switching to nights. My call time isn't until 2 p.m."

"Mason. Don't take this the wrong way. I'd love to. But I haven't had a day off in a long time, it's been a crazy week, and I just need to rest and recharge. You get it, right?"

"I do. But I am only here another week."

"I know. I'm sorry. I can ask Tess to take you around. She'd love it. She's got a huge crush on you."

"She's got a huge crush on a movie star."

"Right."

We walked in silence.

"So what do you suggest I see?"

I thought about it for a moment.

"There are some beautiful hiking trails up

through Carter's Mountain. They pass by Cardinal Lake, which is absolutely breathtaking. If you're into that kind of thing."

He nodded, considering.

"Might be too much exertion considering I'll be shooting after."

"Will you have another day off before you leave?"

"I do, actually. There's one day next week I'm not on the schedule. It's the only day in the entire shoot. Wednesday, I think. Take it off. Spend it with me."

"I'll see what I can do." I pointed left to indicate we needed to turn. "Tess tells me you're going to Switzerland next. How much longer is the shoot?"

"We've got two weeks in Switzerland, then we're done. Jessica is actually getting married in the Alps. It should be fun. Certainly a nice change from the usual location shoot."

"Oh, yes. It must suck to have to travel the globe and see the world."

He stopped and took my hand.

"I didn't mean it like that. I know how fortunate I am. It's just that there are other things to consider. You don't realize how good you have it here. The quiet. The slow pace. The quality of life."

"Well, I guess the grass is always greener.

Because I listen to you and all I can think is how lucky you are to travel around on someone else's dime. To see the world, have adventures, meet new people. Yes, I love my quiet little life, but there's such a thing as too quiet sometimes."

"Too bad we can't pull a *Freaky Friday*."

I laughed as we came to a stop in front of my door. He waited, clearly expecting an invitation. I had already gotten the sense that he expected a lot of things in life. I pulled out my phone and checked the time.

"Listen, I'd invite you up, really, but I've got this luncheon tomorrow and I really need my rest. This gig is going to determine my client list for the next year."

"Got it," he said, taking my phone from my hand. "But take my number. Just in case you change your mind about Sunday."

He punched his number into my phone and handed it back. I took it and offered a small smile before turning and heading inside.

CHAPTER NINE

Jax picked me up in the van at ten the next morning. I'd been showered and dressed for an hour already, unusually nervous given I'd catered dozens of parties. But this was a big one. And I was on my own. Tess had been telling me we needed to hire another person at the counter ever since we launched the catering arm of the business. I'd been in denial. I made a mental note to revisit the issue sooner rather than later.

We rode over to the venue and talked about the setup. Tess and I had agreed Jax would come with me to get everything prepped and ready to go, and then he'd join her. He'd already been in to make sure the day's goods were baked. I pulled down the visor and checked my reflection in the mirror. I'd been obliged to pull a cross between business chic and caterer—not a good mix. But I'd chosen a smart white shift dress with a wide black belt. We'd hired waiters for the affair, so I didn't have to worry about making a mess. I reapplied my lipstick just as Jax parked the car.

The hosts, Vanessa and Felix Branson, were holding the luncheon in the greenhouse in the Mountain Valley Gardens, which exclusively housed flowers and plants indigenous to the north. It was breathtaking. Jax and I just stood there, completely dumb-struck.

"This is the most romantic setting I've ever seen in my entire life. I wish I could stay." Jax looked over at me, silently pleading. I shook my head.

"I promised Tess. I can't leave her alone on a Saturday. That would be insane and cruel. Besides, who are you going to fall in love with? Some fifty-year-old silver fox?"

"I'm not picky," Jax insisted.

We got to work in the kitchen, getting the goods in the ovens and arranging the pastries on trays. Jax made sure every tray was ready and loaded for the waiters before he took off. I would've been lost without him. And Tess. I knew they wouldn't be happy as employees for much longer. I had been talking to my accountant about making them partners, and I decided I'd finally broach the idea with them that week. After I told them I was planning to take Wednesday off.

The waiters arrived and I spent a good ten minutes giving them instructions. Jax and I had already laid out the desserts and I pulled aside two competent servers I knew from past functions and told them how I wanted the sweet table set up. Then I poured myself a mimosa just as Felix Branson walked into the kitchen.

"Katie! So good to see you. Thank you so much for helping us out this morning."

"Mr. Branson. It's my pleasure. Would you like a mimosa?" I offered him my untouched glass and he took it gratefully. I poured myself another.

"It's a beautiful venue, sir. You couldn't have chosen better."

"That was all Vanessa. I just paid for everything." He laughed. "Listen. I'm bringing in some special donors at noon to say a few words. Can I ask you to pass the appetizers, but wait a bit before serving the meal?"

"Absolutely."

"We're eating light, right? My wife mentioned that?"

"She did, sir. We have salads, quiche, and a very light chicken artichoke dish. Perfect for a spring day."

He smiled widely and nodded.

"I'll leave you to it, then. See you out there."

*

At exactly noon, Felix Branson stepped up to the podium. I whispered instructions into my headset for the servers to return to the kitchen and smiled in satisfaction as they all turned on their heels and exited. Like a well-oiled machine. I lifted my glass and took a sip of wine.

"Good morning, thank you all so much for joining Vanessa and me today. Like every year, we hold this luncheon right before the start of the summer season so we can all have a chance to relax and enjoy each other's company before the crowds descend. But this year, we have some very special guests with us. Vanessa?"

Vanessa appeared to join her husband. Tall, svelte, blond, she looked resplendent in a pale pink flowing chiffon summer dress. Felix handed her the mic.

"As my husband said, we have some very special guests. When we heard they were in town, we knew we had to ask them to drop by.

61

Without further ado, Mason Scott and Jessica Thompson!"

I choked on my wine as Mason and Jessica came out and took the podium. Why hadn't he told me? I instinctively looked down and checked my dress, smoothing out the front. I looked back up to see if he'd spotted me, but he and Jessica were exchanging a look before he nodded his head subtly at her. She took the mic.

"Thank you, Vanessa. Thank you, Felix. Thank you so much for inviting us today. Mason and I are so happy to join you all. As you know, we're here in town filming, and looking around this room, I see so many familiar faces. Faces of people who have supported our film and our crew during our stay. As a small thank you, we're going to ask you to stay seated during lunch while we come around, table to table, and chat for a bit. Maybe sign some autographs for your kids?"

The crowd burst into applause as Jessica and Mason stepped down. They separated and, moving in opposite directions, each headed for a table. I called instructions into my headset and the servers emerged with their plates. Mason picked up his head as a server passed, looked around, and finally locked eyes with mine. I grinned and offered a small wave. He flashed me that dazzling smile.

As the hour passed, we both kept busy with our respective duties. The next time I looked up, Jessica was nowhere to be seen, but Mason was making his way over to me. I put down my clipboard and walked to meet him halfway.

"Hey, you," he said.

"Hey, yourself."

"You did an amazing job here today," he said.

"I didn't realize you'd be here."

He shrugged.

"I wanted it to be a surprise. Plus, I knew you were nervous and didn't want to stress you further."

I thought about that.

"Much appreciated," I concluded.

He nodded, took the wine glass from my hand, and took a sip before passing it back. Felix Branson and some friends came over to join us.

"James, Alex, Smith, this is Mason Scott."

Mason smiled and shook hands in turn.

"And this," Mason said, "is Katie Simon, the woman responsible for your meal today."

Felix looked at me with new appreciation.

"I didn't realize you two knew each other," he said. "I will leave you all while I find my wife."

With that, he walked away and Mason turned to dutifully entertain the three men. I was curious to see his charm at work.

"So," James said. "You're the caterer?"

"I am. I hope you enjoyed your lunch."

"It was fantastic. The best food I've had in a long time. I was very impressed."

"I agree," Mason said. "I've been thrilled to have Katie feeding me since I arrived."

"Oh?" Alex said. "Are you his private chef?"

We both laughed.

"No," Mason said. "I'm actually lucky enough to call her a friend."

He leaned in towards them, raising his hand in a stage whisper gesture.

"That way, I don't have to pay for it."

They burst into laughter.

"Pricey, huh?" Alex asked, glancing at me.

"Actually—" I started.

"Let me ask you," Mason interrupted. "If you had food you knew attracted movie stars, what would you charge?"

"Excellent point, Mason," Smith said. "I fully agree. You pay top dollar for the best. It was a pleasure to meet you, Ms. Simon. Do you have a card on you?"

"I absolutely do," I said, pulling a card out from my pocket. Two other hands immediately reached out and I happily obliged them. We said our goodbyes and they moved on.

"Mason!"

He raised his eyebrow and laughed.

"Whatever you're thinking of charging when they call, double it."

"Mason! This is a small town. It doesn't work that way."

"Of course, it does. I know how this crowd thinks. They will pay you a lot of money, and then their guests will call you and pay you even more."

I was about to say something when we were interrupted by a guy with a cell phone and an anxious look.

"Mason? Jessica is waiting in the car. You ready?"

Mason looked around, then back at the driver.

"You know what? I'm going to hang around. You can go."

"You sure?"

"Positive. I'm in good company." He looped his arm through mine.

"Okay, then. I'll pick you up at 1:30 tomorrow."

"Why did you do that?" I asked as the driver walked away. "Now you're stuck here."

"I wouldn't call it stuck. Besides, they've finished lunch. How much longer do you have to work?"

"Through dessert."

"Oh. Okay, then. I'm heading to the bar. I'll catch you soon."

"You're crazy, you know that? You'll be swamped."

Mason looked around the room, carefully surveying the crowd.

"There were a couple of women under 40," he said thoughtfully.

I stared at him.

"We're just friends, right?" he asked wickedly.

"Yes, we're just friends."

He shrugged and walked away. We were just friends. That had been my choice. And it had been the smart choice.

Right?

*

By the time I was ready to pack it up, I was out of business cards. Word had spread like wildfire through the crowd and as Jax and I loaded the van, my heart was as light as my step. Despite my overwhelming fatigue, I was positively euphoric.

I went back inside to find Mason. He wasn't at the bar so I scanned the room until I saw him sitting with a pretty brunette, around my age, at a far table in the corner. I contemplated not going over there, but it struck me as incredibly rude to leave without him. Especially since he'd stayed behind for me. But at the same time, it looked like he'd possibly found another ride and might be grateful if I just disappeared.

I was standing there, wondering what to do, when he lifted his head and saw me. He flashed that smile and instantly stood. The brunette turned slightly to look at me and then smiled at him, reaching out her hand. They shook, and Mason made his way over.

"I'm sorry," I said. "I didn't mean to interrupt. If you want to stay. . .she seems. . .nice."

"Don't be silly. We were just talking. Let's go."

I led him through the kitchen out the back way and Jax's jaw dropped to the floor when we stepped into the parking lot.

"Uh, Katie. You didn't mention—"

"Jax, this is Mason Scott. Mason, this is Jax. Jax works with me. I'd be lost without him."

Jax walked over and shook Mason's hand reverentially. I almost burst out laughing. Mason was obviously used to it and tried to engage Jax in conversation, I guess to distract him.

"Oh, yeah? How long have you two worked together?" he asked.

"I have no idea," Jax said.

Mason burst out laughing.

"Jax, man. Relax. I'm just a guy."

"No. You're not. You're a god."

I rolled my eyes.

"Jax. Stop it. We're giving Mason a ride. You can't act like this."

Jax snapped to attention. He swallowed, ran his hand through his hair, and tried on a casual smile. It kind of worked.

"Okay, then. Everyone in," he said.

I slid onto the front bench seat between Jax and Mason, even though Jax probably would've forfeited his entire week's pay if I'd had Mason take the middle.

"Where you headed?" I asked Mason, not wanting to assume anything.

"The hotel, I guess."

"You have no plans?"

He shook his head. I turned to Jax.

"You can drop us at my place."

Jax squeaked. It was a tiny squeak, but we all heard it. Mason shook with suppressed laughter beside me.

"You sure?" Mason asked.

"Yes. You're off, I'm off. It might be the only

chance we have to hang out."

"You must be exhausted."

I shrugged.

"I'll sleep tomorrow."

"I'm in."

CHAPTER TEN

As soon as we stepped into the apartment, I kicked off my shoes and dropped my bag, not even stopping as I made my way to the couch. I plopped down and put up my feet, letting my head fall back as I closed my eyes.

"I can't even imagine how exhausted you are. You sure you don't want me to go?" Mason asked.

I lifted my head and cracked open one eye.

"What I want is for you to order a pizza. Dial 555-5535. I don't care what's on it."

He laughed and reached for his phone, doing as asked. He loaded on the meat toppings and my heart sang a little song of joy. When he tacked on the fries, I thought I'd die of happiness. He hung up and sat on the couch, at the opposite end from where I was.

"Pass me your feet. I have sisters. I'm really good at this," he promised.

I swiveled around and rested my feet in his lap. He got to work and my eyes immediately closed again. He wasn't kidding. He was saying something about the scene they were going to shoot the next day but my mind was wandering. I found it very difficult to focus on anything except the warm sensations spreading through my body.

"Katie! Katie, wake up. The pizza is here. I don't know the code to buzz him in."

I sat up straight, groggy and confused. I looked at Mason and he handed me the phone. I punched six, hung up, and rubbed my eyes.

"Did I fall asleep?" I asked.

"You did. For a good forty-five minutes. No worries. I was snooping."

I jumped up, alarmed.

"I'm kidding," he said as he went to answer the knock at the door.

When the delivery guy saw Mason standing there, his jaw dropped.

"You're. . .you're. . ."

"Yes, I am. What do I owe you?"

"Oh, dude. The pizza's on me. I can't wait to tell the guys back at the shop."

Mason reached into his pocket and pulled out a fifty-dollar bill, handing it to the guy.

"Then consider this a tip."

"Will you sign it?" the kid asked eagerly.

Mason laughed and I handed him a Sharpie I had in a mug on the hallway table. He signed the bill for the kid and handed it over. The kid stared at it with an awed expression for a full thirty seconds before folding it carefully and tucking it into his shirt pocket.

"Cool," he said.

Mason closed the door and turned to hand me the pizza box and fries. I made my way back to the living room while he went into the kitchen to fetch some drinks. He emerged with a bottle of wine and two glasses.

"This okay?" he asked.

"It's fine, but I may pass out on you."

He came over and sat down beside me on the floor, in front of the coffee table.

"I feel like a kid again," he said.

"You're telling me you haven't eaten pizza on the floor since you were a kid?" I extracted a slice from the box and took a bite.

"There's a lot of things I haven't done since I was a kid."

I glanced at him.

"How long have you been acting?"

"Since I was about eleven."

"Wow. That's like, what? Fifteen years?"

"Nineteen."

I whistled.

"Looking good, my friend."

He burst out laughing.

"And it's been that long since you've had a normal life?"

"Pretty much. I landed a series my first year out. It wasn't a hit or anything, but it opened the door for me for a lot of guest appearances on different series. Then I got my first indie movie, and the rest, as they say, is history. First lead role in a blockbuster was seven years ago."

I was silent as I contemplated this, what kind of existence it must've meant for him.

"I take it you're not a big movie fan?" he asked.

"Why? Because I didn't recognize you? I like movies, it's just the whole celebrity thing I'm not into. No offense."

"No offense? Please. You're the perfect audience."

I reached for a second slice and Mason scooped a handful of fries onto my plate. I dipped one in ketchup and popped it in my mouth.

"God, Katie, you don't know how amazing this is. To just be here, with you, eating pizza. Thank you."

I raised my eyebrows in acknowledgment and kept eating.

"What made you get into acting?" I asked him after a while.

"From the time I was really young, I liked pretending to be someone else. That's the best way to describe it. I love the ability to crawl out of my own skin and into someone else's."

"But you're not a method actor?"

"No." He laughed. "Not at all. It's easy for me to just slip in and out of the role. And I love the escape. Don't get me wrong, it's work. But I love it. I could never give it up. I just wish I could slow it down. Have more moments like these."

"Why can't you?"

"There's this fear. Out of sight, out of mind. If I disappeared, they'd forget about me."

I snorted.

"It's true," he insisted.

I finished my glass of wine and Mason reached for the bottle to give me a refill. Between the day, the wine, the pizza, I was feeling pretty drowsy. But I also didn't want him to go, so I struggled to keep my eyes open.

"What about you?" he asked. "Have you always wanted to own a bakery?"

I laughed loudly.

"No. I didn't think I'd come back after

university. I figured I'd find my way out in the world. I mean, I love it here, but inheriting the bakery was not in the cards. It wasn't a surprise, but it wasn't necessarily my plan, if you know what I mean."

"I do. Any regrets that you didn't sell it?"

"None. None at all. I love baking. I love making people happy with food. I guess I just wish—"

"You wish what?"

I shook my head.

"Tell me."

"I wish I could expand. I've been so happy since we started catering, but I want more. I want my cakes to be known. I want people saying, 'I need Katie Simon to do my wedding cake.'"

Mason was silent and I felt like an idiot. I'd never even told Tess that before. I was trying to figure out how to take it back. It sounded so vain, but it wasn't about me. It was about the cake. It was about the work.

"Sounds silly? Vain?" I asked.

"Not at all. And more, I think you could do it. You're amazing."

I smiled and got up from the floor, brushing the pizza crumbs from my dress. I drained my glass as he stood up and took a seat back on the couch. I put my glass down.

"I'm just going to change out of this dress. I'll be right back."

He nodded a picked up a magazine off the coffee table, flipping through the pages as I left the room. I walked into my bedroom and peeled off the dress, fishing a pair of sweatpants and a T-shirt out of a clean laundry basket and pulling them on. I turned back to rejoin him in the living room, but I moved too suddenly and everything went kind of blurry. I sat down on the edge of the bed, waiting for the moment to pass. Too much wine on too little sleep. I glanced at the pillow. *Would it really hurt to lay down for a minute?*

*

When I opened my eyes, light was streaming in through the window. I ran my hand over my face, confused, and slowly turned over to read the clock on my bedside table. It was 9:30 a.m. I shot straight up.

"Holy shit!" I yelled.

I heard a crash from the living room which made me jump further.

"Who's there?" I called, which was ridiculous. What if it was a burglar? What did I intend to do about it? I searched frantically for my phone but when I looked up, Mason was standing in my doorway, rubbing his eyes.

"Hey," he said.

"Oh my god. I must have fallen asleep. I'm so sorry. Worst host ever." I laughed nervously.

"Please. I fell asleep waiting for you. Worst guest ever."

I stood up and my hand immediately went to my hair.

"Stop it," he said quietly. "You look adorable."

I rolled my eyes.

"You want me to go?" he asked. "I had no intention of spending the night."

"What time do you have to be on set?"

"Two o'clock."

"Stay. We'll have a lazy breakfast. I'll make French toast."

"Sounds divine. Would you, uh, happen to have a spare toothbrush?"

I laughed.

"You mean even movie stars wake up with bad breath? Yes. Top drawer in the bathroom vanity."

He gave me a quick salute and turned on his heel. I walked over and looked in the mirror. *Adorable, my ass.* I was mortified. I quickly changed my clothes—leggings and an oversized sweatshirt—and ran my fingers through my hair. Sometimes, the whole stick-straight thing worked in my favour.

CHAPTER ELEVEN

After a nice relaxed breakfast—which Mason enjoyed immensely—it was already nearing noon. I knew he had to get back to the hotel before his call time and even though I'd been anticipating a day of solo relaxation, I was sorry to see him go.

"Have a great day off," he said when I walked him to the door.

"Thanks. There's a definite bubble bath in my future."

"Listen. Why don't you come by set tomorrow in the afternoon? We start at three."

"I don't know. The last time I was there—"

"I looked like an idiot," Mason interrupted. "You have nothing to worry about. I promise.

If you're worried, bring a cake."

"A cake?"

He looked a little sheepish as he opened the door.

"Yeah. It's Mark the grip's birthday."

I smacked him over the head as he ducked out of my apartment, laughing as he took off down the stairs. I closed the door and walked slowly back to the living room. Sinking into the couch, I realized I'd pretty much spent the night with a movie star.

*

I was loading the bread onto the shelves early Monday morning when Tess rushed in, apologizing profusely for being late. I checked the time and saw it was almost seven.

"Leave the door unlocked," I said. "We open in three minutes."

"Shit! I'm so sorry, Katie."

"It's okay. Go wash up and get your apron on. I'll handle the front."

Within minutes, there was a line to the door of people waiting for their coffee and croissant. Or donut. Or whatever else they fancied that morning. By the time Jax came in at eleven, I'd already loaded more trays into the oven. It was an exceptionally busy morning, but right after the lunch crowd left, things quieted down.

"You taking off?" Jax asked.

"In a few minutes," I said. "I wanted to talk to you two about something."

They threw each other a look.

"You slept with the movie star," Jax said.

I rolled my eyes as I grabbed my notebook from the back counter. Thankfully, neither of them noticed. I didn't want to start this conversation off on a sour note. I remembered my plan and smiled instead, turning to face them.

"No, I wanted to talk about the bakery."

"You're going to hire someone!" Tess screamed.

"No. Well, yes, but that's not what I wanted to talk about."

They both started giggling at the idea of help in the kitchen and behind the counter, so I let them enjoy themselves for a moment before moving on. When Tess started fantasizing about increasing her break time, I decided to cut in.

"Okay. Enough. Listen to me. This is serious. I've been talking to my accountant and I've been thinking about the future, and, well, I think it's time for you both to come in as partners. . .if you're interested."

The laughter stopped and both heads

snapped in my direction. Jax got up from the stool he was sitting on and Tess slowly wiped her hands on her apron. They were both eyeing me like I was an alien.

"You're not interested?" I asked.

"Of course, I'm interested," Jax croaked. Tess just stared at me, mouth agape.

"Well, we can sit down with the guy and he'll walk us through all the details. I couldn't do this without you, and you're both more than employees at this point. It's time. And I want to do this before we hire an additional person."

Tess slowly walked over and then threw her arms around me. She squeezed me so tight I thought I'd pass out.

"This won't ruin our friendship, will it?" she asked.

I laughed.

"No. I can't see much changing. You both already tell me what to do anyway. And I want to concentrate on expansion. I'd love to do a line of cakes. Speaking of which, I better go grab the one I made this morning from the walk-in."

"I saw that," Jax said. "Impressive. Who's it for?"

"I'm going to visit Mason on set today. It's a crew member's birthday. I made a little cake."

Jax snorted. Tess squealed.

"Can I come? Please, can I come?"

I glanced at Jax and he nodded.

"I can spare you for an hour during the afternoon lull. Just be sure to be back by five."

Tess jumped up and clapped her hands. Then she took my hand and led me toward the kitchen.

"Come, show me this masterpiece."

*

With Tess's help, I managed to get the cake out to the car. It was huge. I wasn't sure how big the crew was, and I didn't want to take any chances. I'd opted for a sheet cake but then decided to make it three-layer, each one a little smaller than the last. On top, I'd created fondant dolly tracks with a camera set up in the middle. It was gorgeous.

When we arrived on location, the same guy was standing on the sidewalk, a walkie-talkie hanging from his belt. He grinned as he saw us approach and rushed over to help.

"Hi," I said. "I'm here to see Mason Scott."

"Yup. We're expecting you, Katie. Follow me."

Tess looked over, completely unable to contain her shit-eating grin. She did a little skip step as we followed the guy towards set. He put out a hand to quiet us just as the director yelled "Action!" and we both stood still, watching Mason and Jessica Thompson go through their scene. It was a short scene and they were arguing about something. Tess was completely enraptured.

As I stood there watching, everything else around me fell away. The first thing I noticed was my heart speeding up, followed by some pretty serious dry mouth. *What the hell was going on?* Mason reached out to touch Jessica's face, and my belly did a quick flip-flop. I felt my face get red as I imagined him touching me that way.

It was ridiculous. We'd spent time together. We'd agreed to be friends. He'd stayed the night and we hadn't even kissed. What had changed? Something had changed. There was no denying it. I was suddenly grateful he was only in town a few more days. I'd find some excuse to get out of seeing him on Wednesday.

As they leaned in for a make-up kiss, Tess squeezed my hand and whispered in my ear, "Their chemistry is insane."

That was it. I was just feeling the chemistry they were sharing on set. He was just that good an actor. The director yelled "Cut!" and it was like a swarm of bees descended on Mason and Jessica. After a few moments, they started to scatter and as Mason made his way over to us, someone appeared to take the cake out of my hands.

"You must be Tess," Mason said, taking her hand and kissing it. I thought she'd pass out.

"Um. Yes? I think," she muttered, blushing furiously.

I watched him as he smiled calmly at her, waiting for her to collect herself. Suddenly, my baseball-cap-wearing friend was in full wardrobe and make-up and larger than life. Even I couldn't help but stare at him. I was breathless and glad he'd chosen to turn the charm on Tess. I wasn't sure what I would've done.

"Katie said it would be okay if I came," Tess said, still flustered.

"It's absolutely fine. I'm glad she brought you. I hear you're a big movie fan. Want someone to take you on a tour? They're setting up for a different shot, so there's time."

Her eyes lit up and Mason called someone named Nick over.

"You look familiar," Tess said. Nick laughed.

"I live here, Tess. They were hiring local crew, so I figured, why not?"

"Nick Felton?" Tess said.

He nodded.

"Oh my god." Tess was looking back and

forth between Mason and Nick.

I almost burst out laughing. She was clearly torn. On one hand, there was Mason Scott, but on the other hand, Nick was pretty hot himself. And attainable. She slowly tore her eyes away from Mason and walked towards Nick.

"You wouldn't mind showing me around?" she asked, suddenly all coy.

"It would be my pleasure," Nick said.

Mason and I watched as the two of them walked away.

"Don't forget you've only got about 45 minutes, Tess!" I called.

"Yup," she called over her shoulder. "I'll see you tomorrow."

Mason turned to me and my breath caught again.

"Hey, you," he said quietly.

"Hey," I breathed.

He looked at me, head cocked as he studied me.

"Something is different," he said. *Crap.*

"Not sure what you mean."

"I don't know. You look different."

I turned my head before he could see me blush.

"Do I get a tour?" I asked. "Or are you too busy? You must be too busy."

"I've got a few minutes," he said.

He took my hand and led me towards the craft services table, grabbing a donut as we walked by.

"Not as good as your stuff, of course, but beggars can't be choosers."

I laughed nervously, once more wondering what made today different. I felt like a schoolgirl, not a full-grown woman who owned and ran a successful business. Fine, I didn't have a lot of experience with men, but I had had a few relationships. I may never have been in love, but I'd certainly been in lust. I'd never felt like this before.

I tried to listen as he walked me around, showing me the makeup and wardrobe trailers, the props department, and the office where the second assistant director was busy at his computer, shouting instructions into a cell phone. But all the while, I was watching his mouth as he spoke. The way his muscles moved along his jawline. The way he passed his hand through his hair. I tried to regulate my breathing as we approached his trailer.

"I've got three more minutes. Come see inside."

He stepped up and pulled me along behind him. I took a tentative step up and followed him, pulling the door closed behind me. I looked around, barely taking in the swank furnishings and gorgeous fruit plate on the table.

"So whenever I have downtime—"

Before he could finish the thought, I kissed him. I put my hands on either side of his face, drew him in towards me as I stepped up on my tiptoes, and kissed him. He blinked for a moment, standing still, and then wrapped one arm around my waist, drawing me in closer. I melted against him as he returned the kiss, my lips parting to make way for him. I wound my arms around his neck, closing my eyes and losing myself in the moment; not even questioning what had gotten into me, just enjoying it. He let go of my waist and held my head with both hands as we came up for air. I opened my eyes to see him gazing at me with wonder before his mouth closed over mine again.

There was a sharp knock at the door.

"Mason! On set!"

Mason drew back, staring at me as if for the first time.

"Shit. I've got to go."

"It's okay."

"It's not okay. What the hell just happened?"

I shrugged.

"I wanted to kiss you."

"Well, don't get me wrong, I'm very pleased

about that, but I thought you said—"

"Don't over-think it. We on for Wednesday?"

"Yes. Absolutely."

As if on cue, there was another knock. More insistent this time.

"I'll see you then," he said, kissing me quickly before walking out the door.

CHAPTER TWELVE

The next day, I was serving at the bakery when the phone rang. I called for Tess to get it as I rang the customer out. I heard her answer the phone and when I turned to see who it was, she was grinning from ear to ear. She held out the phone.

"It's for you," she said in a sing-song voice.

I rolled my eyes as I wiped my hands on the apron and took the receiver from her.

"Hello?" I said.

"Hey, it's me," Mason said.

"Hey, you."

"We still on for tomorrow?"

"We are. I've got to take care of some business in the morning. Why don't you meet me outside the Front Street Café at one?"

"I'll be there. Katie—"

Before he could say anything else, I heard a loud voice calling his name in the background.

"You've got to go. Park that thought and tell me tomorrow. I'll see you then," I said. I hung up the phone feeling a lot less brave than I sounded.

When I walked back to the counter, Tess eyed me curiously. She started pulling out trays and stacking pastries towards the front, getting ready for the afternoon crowd.

"Who are you meeting tomorrow morning?" she asked, trying to sound all nonchalant.

"Ted. The accountant. We're going to sit down and draw up some papers. I'll bring them in with me on Thursday when I come back. Then you both—" I glanced over at Jax. "Can have a chance to go through them yourselves."

Jax ran over and gave me a quick hug.

"This is going to be great, Katie. I promise."

"I know it will. Frankly, it's a relief to me. I feel like I've been carrying this for so long. I haven't had a vacation in forever. I'm thinking —"

"You can take time off as soon as we hire," Tess said firmly. I laughed.

"Getting the hang of partnership already, are

you?" I grinned.

The bell jingled as a customer walked through the front door, quickly followed by two more. I checked the time—it was closing in on noon. I flashed a brief smile at my soon-to-be partners and we got to work on the afternoon rush.

*

On Wednesday morning, the sun was shining in a clear sky and by ten a.m., it was already hotter than usual. I was glad to have chosen a light sundress with spaghetti straps. It was periwinkle blue and fell just below my knees. It was one of the most flattering dresses I owned and my wearing it had absolutely nothing to do with the fact that I was meeting Mason afterward.

I approached Ted's office, a small, two-story, commercially-zoned house that he shared with another accountant and a lawyer. It was a nice setup and I'd come to Ted through Nate, the lawyer, who'd taken care of my grandmother's affairs. Ted was in his mid-fifties, super smart about money, and had guided me through all the financial aspects of the business since I took over. With his help, I was turning a profit year over year. When I'd approached him about bringing Jax and Tess on as partners, he'd thought it was brilliant.

Now, as I walked into his office, I noticed a frown on his face as he went over some papers. I sat down quietly, not wanting to disturb him but also feeling a little sick at the idea the frown might've been directed at my bank statements. After a few moments, I cleared my throat. He looked up immediately.

"Katie! Sorry. I didn't even hear you come in."

I gave him a nervous glance and gestured vaguely towards his papers.

"Upsetting information?" I asked.

He nodded solemnly.

"Unfortunately, yes. I've been going through this all morning and, well, I just—"

"But Ted, I just told Jax and Tess that everything was good, that we were going to—"

"Katie," he laughed. "These aren't your papers. I'm sorry. I probably should've led with that."

I was so relieved I couldn't even be upset at the misunderstanding. An awkward laugh escaped as I ran my hand through my hair. I straightened up in my seat and tried to look professional.

"Okay, then. Let's start again."

I spent the next two hours going over

everything in detail with him, making sure I understood all the finer points so I could explain them to Jax and Tess and answer any questions they might have. Naturally, it would've been ideal for us all to be present, but given we were the only three people keeping the bakery running, it had been kind of impossible. I made a mental note to bring up the idea of closing one day a week.

When Ted cleared his throat, I realized I'd drifted off a little. I gave him my full attention and silently thanked my lucky stars I had him. I could wrap my head around the money, but I preferred to focus on baking. I considered myself more of an artist than a businessperson. Tess had the business mind. I'd be glad to offset some of this stuff once things were settled.

When we were done, I stood up and thanked Ted profusely for all the hard work he'd put into the deal. I took two copies of the paperwork and put them in my purse, thankful I'd chosen an oversized tote for the day. As I left his office, I realized one o'clock had been kind of an ambiguous meeting time. Were we having lunch? Was this post-lunch? Unsure and unwilling to spend the afternoon hangry, I stopped off on my way to the cafe for a quick bite at my favourite diner. I was in and out within forty-five minutes and was priding myself on my punctuality when I saw Mason standing at our meeting spot. He was early.

CHAPTER THIRTEEN

I ignored the pounding of my heart in my ears as I came to a stop before Mason, leaving at least a few feet between us. Even so, I was sure he could hear the *thump thump*. I smiled and leaned in for a quick, one-armed hug before resuming a safe distance.

"Hey," he said. "You look great."

I glanced down, self-consciously scanning my outfit despite the fact I'd spent far too much time that morning picking it out.

"Thanks," I mumbled. "Any idea what you'd like to do today? You've got one day to see the sights."

"I was thinking about that hike you mentioned the other day. Would you be into that?" he asked.

I considered it for a moment before turning to him.

"I'd love to, but I'm not exactly dressed appropriately for hiking. Can we make a quick stop at my apartment so I can change?"

"Sure thing."

We fell into step beside each other as we walked towards my building. Neither of us was in any great rush, and it was far too hot to move quickly in any case. The silence, at first comfortable, grew awkward as we walked.

"So," I said, grasping for the first topic of conversation I could think of, "how come the great Mason Scott doesn't have a girlfriend?"

I wanted to slap myself upside the head. Could I have possibly come up with a dumber question? It was probably the first thing every reporter asked him, too. I was trying to find a lighthearted way to take it back, but as I was struggling, he started speaking.

"Well, to tell you the truth, I just haven't met the right person. This is a tough business. I'm in the spotlight all the time. Cameras follow me everywhere." He glanced around. "Except here, apparently. In any case, it's a lot to ask someone else to go through. I've dated a few actresses, but really. . .I just haven't met the right person. It would have to be someone really special to risk all the accompanying madness."

"Wow," I said. "That sounds. . .lonely."

He laughed.

"I'm not looking for pity. Poor little rich boy. No, I'm just saying, it's a catch-22. And even if I did find the right person, and we did decide to make a go of it, how can a relationship survive that kind of scrutiny?"

I couldn't think of anything to say to that, so I said nothing.

"What about you?" he asked. "No boyfriend in the picture?"

I shook my head.

"Nope. Obligatory high school romance, followed by a lengthy college mistake. I've been pretty much on my own since then."

"Huh."

I was dying to question that 'huh' but bit my tongue.

"Do you date? I mean, such a small town, is there enough. . .variety?"

I burst out laughing.

"You sound like an overanxious mother. Truthfully, no, there isn't enough variety, as you put it. But it doesn't matter because pretty much all my time is devoted to the bakery."

"And the catering."

"Well, the catering is new. And thanks to

you, we've got a great summer lined up."

"Mark's cake was amazing, by the way. The whole cast and crew were talking about it."

I smiled shyly.

"Yeah. And the cakes."

"Even without the dating, you still have time for all of it? I mean, no offense, but you already seem pretty worn out." He smiled. "You did pass out on me the other night."

I bumped him with my shoulder playfully and he laughed as he veered off-course for a moment.

"So, that's where I was this morning. I've spoken to Tess and Jax and I'm bringing them in as partners in the business. I couldn't do it without them, and sooner or later they'd smarten up and leave me. This way, they get a slice of the pie—pun intended—and I get a little breathing room."

"To bake cakes."

"Among other things."

"Like?"

"I don't know, maybe travel a little? I'd like to see some places."

"You did mention travel. Okay, so this can work out really well for you. That's great, Katie."

By this time, we'd arrived at my building, and as I worked my key in the lock, Mason placed his hand on the small of my back. It was a casual gesture, but it sent electric sparks up my spine. It took all my willpower not to straighten up, not to show any sign it had affected me. But the truth was, it had been a long time since I'd been with a man and for the first time in a while, I was really feeling it. I swallowed as I pulled the key out of the lock and pushed the door open. He followed close behind, only dropping his hand at the last moment.

*

We entered the apartment and I dropped my keys and bag on the hallway table. Mason closed the door behind us and kicked off his shoes.

"I'll only be a minute." I made my way towards my bedroom.

"Take your time," he called.

I walked into my room and pulled out a T-shirt and a pair of shorts. I took off my sandals and hunted around for a pair of socks.

"Is it okay if I grab a drink?" Mason said. It sounded like he was already in the kitchen.

"Sure thing. There's some iced tea in the fridge."

I stood in front of my dresser, grimacing at

100

myself in the mirror as I struggled with the zipper on the back of my dress. It was just out of reach. Mason passed by and I called out to him.

"Can you just help me with this?" I asked.

He walked over and put his drink down on the dresser. I swallowed as his cold fingers reached for the zipper, and I couldn't help but shiver as I felt them slide down my back. I looked at his reflection in the mirror and our eyes caught. We just stood there, staring at each other in the mirror as his hand rested on my bare skin. My breathing became erratic and he trailed his fingers lightly back up my spine, pausing at the base of my neck. He watched me, waiting for me to stop him, before his hand continued to my shoulder, pushing the strap of my dress down. We both watched it fall, his hand close behind as he ran it over my upper arm.

He checked my face once more before bending his head and gently kissing me, right beneath my ear. A small moan escaped and I relaxed against his back. His left hand moved up and slid the strap off my other shoulder. We both stood there, his hands resting on both my upper arms, watching each other in the mirror. It was the most erotic thing I'd ever experienced and the heat was rapidly spreading through my body.

He leaned in once more and kissed a trail along the back of my neck, from one shoulder to the other. He ran his hands down my arms and I felt the dress slide down my body and collect in a pool at my feet. I glanced up and caught him staring at me in the mirror.

"Katie," he breathed.

I smiled shyly as his hand skimmed lightly over my breast. I closed my eyes, arched my back, and sighed, at which point he turned me around and I felt his mouth land on mine. His kiss was gentle at first, only increasing in intensity when I wound my arms around his neck, pressing my breasts into his chest. This kiss was different from the previous two. More insistent, bordering on urgent. I felt almost wicked, standing there in my panties while he was still fully dressed, but I didn't care. In fact, it was an incredible turn-on. And judging by the evidence against my leg, he was pretty turned on, too.

I ran my hands through his hair while his ran paths up and down my body. He was exploring every inch, his open palms against my back, along my waist, his hands grabbing at my hips to pull me in closer. I responded by eliminating every inch of space between us, repositioning myself so I could slowly grind up against him. I felt rather than heard the growl that started deep in his chest.

"Come to the bed," he whispered in my ear, his hands rounding my ass and trying to lift me.

I shook my head and turned around, bracing my hands on the dresser.

"Right here," I said.

He caught my eye in the mirror and I watched as he unbuckled his belt and dropped his pants, but not before retrieving his wallet from the back pocket. He pulled out a condom and rolled it on, then stepped towards me and wrapped his hands around me, covering my breasts as he stared into my eyes. I tried to keep them open, to watch him as his thumbs ran over my nipples, raising them to stiff peaks. I tried not to cry out as he nibbled on my ear, whispering about the feel of my breasts against his skin.

I bent over and raised myself on my tiptoes, trying to press myself against him, coaxing him inside. But he resisted, sliding one hand down to my stomach, slowly, easing it between my legs. This time the cry escaped as I bit my lip and felt him explore.

"You're so wet," he whispered. "Please, let me make you come."

"I want you, Mason. Now."

He sighed, powerless, and took hold of my hips. I felt his foot nudge my ankle, pushing my legs farther apart. I pressed my chest against the dresser, keeping my eyes glued to our reflection, and watched as he slid into me slowly from behind.

"Oh, god, Katie," he groaned.

He closed his eyes and I watched his jaw work as he moved slowly in and out of me, echoing the restraint he must have been exercising. I got up on my tiptoes and rocked backwards, into him, urging him to speed up.

"Katie, I'm trying to—"

"Shut up and fuck me."

He needed no further encouragement. He kept one hand on my hip as his other traveled back up to my breast, which he gently kneaded while increasing the speed of his thrusts. The most delicious sensation ran down my body, culminating between my thighs as he continued to fuck me while rolling my nipple between his thumb and forefinger. I dropped one hand between my legs and found my clit, rubbing slowly, then frantically, as he really started to drive into me.

"Oh, fuck. Katie, that is so hot. I can't—"

His head dropped against my back as his hips snapped against me. I reached down beneath us, gently cupping him as I felt him ride out his orgasm. His hands came to rest on my hips, his face still pressed against me as his breathing slowly regulated. He straightened up and I turned around, hopping up on the dresser to face him. I could feel the ear-splitting grin break out across my face. He just stared at me, incredulous.

"Katie. I. . .I . . . Well, let's just say when I imagined us having sex—and yes, I imagined us having sex—I always thought it would be kind of . . .sweet. I did not expect that. Holy shit."

He burst out into nervous laughter as he considered me with new eyes. I blushed under his scrutiny and looked down at my feet.

"I've never done that before," I said quietly.

"Excuse me? Never done what?"

"Had sex standing up."

"What?"

I shrugged.

"It's true. You're right. By all accounts, sex with me should have been . . .sweet, as you put it. But there we were, and I can't even remember the last time I had sex, and on top of everything else, you're a goddamn movie star. So I figured, why not?"

Mason burst out laughing. A deep, body-shaking laugh that started in his belly and rolled off him like pure joy. He leaned over and kissed me, then scooped me off the dresser and carried me over to the bed. He laid me down, then crawled up next to me. He planted another soft kiss on my lips, brushed the hair from my face, and looked me deep in the eyes.

"Fuck the hike. I think we've enough to keep us busy here."

CHAPTER FOURTEEN

"I thought you wanted to explore the sights," I said, sitting up and trying to catch my breath.

Mason paused as he considered me.

"Oh. Well. I think all the sights I want to explore are right here."

With that, he dipped his head and ran the tip of his tongue lightly across my breast.

I tried to get comfortable with zero success. He looked up, a quizzical expression on his face. He pushed himself up on his elbow so he was once again above me.

"What's wrong?"

"Can we get under the covers?"

He laughed and ran his finger along my jaw, stopping at my chin and tilting my head so I was forced to look him in the eye.

"Feeling shy all of a sudden?" he asked, a mischievous gleam in his eye.

I blushed.

"I mean, I've never even had sex with the lights on," I admitted.

He shook his head, still laughing.

"Nope. Not gonna work. I've seen this Katie. No going back. Clearly, this is the Katie who wants to fool around with me."

He gently pushed me back on the bed and when his tongue once again made contact with my nipple, I gave into him completely. I wound my fingers through his hair as he worked his way down my body, kissing, nipping, licking. He ducked under my leg, positioning himself between my thighs. I sighed and lay my head back on the pillow, bringing my knees up as he slid his hands under my ass.

His tongue was magic. I should've known from the way he kissed. I let go of his head and gripped the blanket beneath me, digging my heels into the bed as I tried to fight the orgasm I already felt building. It had been so long, and the sex had been so hot, and before I could even take in another breath, I felt the thunder rolling through me.

"Oh, *fuck*," I cried.

Mason grabbed my ass as he gently swirled his tongue, my thighs spread wide to accommodate him. I felt control slipping away as his mouth closed on my clitoris. I cried out as I raised my hips off the bed, the orgasm taking control of my body and sending electric currents down my limbs. He refused to stop, and I almost pulled away when I felt the second orgasm crash over me.

"*Oh, FUCK!*"

Mason chuckled as he lifted his head and looked at me across the expanse of belly and breasts. I couldn't catch my breath. He gave me a quick squeeze then crawled back up to give me a slow, lingering kiss. I melted into that kiss, putting my hand behind his neck to keep him close as he tried to pull away. I felt him smile against my mouth and I snuggled in close. When I finally broke away, he was still smiling.

"That was amazing," I said.

"It certainly was."

I lay back and stared up at the ceiling while Mason traced lines down my side with his fingertips. I tried to process what had just happened, what was *still* happening, but it seemed too surreal.

*

I woke up a while later, Mason lying beside me and stroking my hair gently. I smiled up at him and moved to pull up the sheet. He grabbed my wrist.

"Nope. Enjoying the view."

I rolled my eyes before covering my face with my hands. He pulled them away and leaned in to kiss me.

"Have a nice nap?" he asked.

I may have purred.

"I hate to disturb you, but I'm getting kind of hungry. Worked up a bit of an appetite earlier," he said.

I laughed and rolled over, grabbing his shirt and pulling it over my head as I got out of bed. He sat up and eyed me appreciatively with a look that made me want to crawl right back in.

"Don't even think about it," he said. "I'm not touching you until I know there's food."

"What would you like?"

"What have you got?"

"Nothing really. We're going to order in. Unless you'd rather go out?"

He shook his head furiously.

"I just want to fuel up and then have more Katie."

That sounded like an excellent plan to me. I went to fetch the menus.

*

By midnight, it was time for Mason to leave. There was nothing I'd have liked more than for him to spend the night. But I knew that in two days, he'd be gone. Right now, it was a one-night stand. Spending the night would bring it to a whole other level.

As I watched him dress, I mentally prepared myself for the fact I'd likely never see him again. I silently willed him to slow down as he raised his arms over his head to pull on his shirt. The same shirt that had been on my body just a few hours earlier. I felt the now-familiar tingling between my legs and wondered how long it would be until I was with someone again. How could I go back to the farm now that I'd see Paris?

As if reading my mind and wanting to leave me with one more memento, he bent down and kissed me. Deeply. I closed my eyes and parted my lips, but left my hands by my side. He pulled away but stayed close, gazing at me with an expression I couldn't read.

"Come to the wrap party Friday night," he said.

My heart stopped.

"Really?"

"Yeah. For sure. I meant to ask earlier but got distracted."

"Can I bring Tess?"

"You can bring Tess," he laughed. "Jax, too."

I opened my mouth to thank him, then paused for a beat. He didn't miss it.

"What's wrong?"

"Nothing's wrong. I'd love to go. But don't invite me because you think this will happen again." He opened his mouth to speak but I put up my hand. "This was amazing. Best sex ever. You're incredible. We're . . .incredible. But you're leaving. And I can't risk—"

He kissed me.

"Katie. Stop. I don't expect you to fuck me in the bathroom at the wrap party. I'm asking you to come because I like you. We have talked pretty extensively about our respective dating situations. I think we're pretty clear on that front. You don't have the time; I don't have the inclination."

He stopped, swallowed, then continued.

"Don't get me wrong. If things were different, fuck. I wouldn't let you out of my sight. But I see who you are. I would never bring you into my world."

I smiled, mentally tucking away that 'if things were different' comment for scrutiny later before giving him a quick kiss. It was all I needed to hear. I walked him to the door, gave him a hug, and watched him walk away.

CHAPTER FIFTEEN

"We're doing what now?"

Tess looked from me to Jax back to me again to make sure she heard properly. I nodded my head. Jax was speechless.

"We're going to the wrap party?" she repeated.

I nodded again. I wasn't sure what else I had to do to convince her. I glanced over at Jax. Still shell-shocked. I suppressed a smile.

"We're catering the wrap party?" he asked, finally finding some words.

"No," I said patiently. "We are invited. As guests. To eat and drink and dance with the movie stars."

They looked at each other and burst into

hysterics. Simultaneous chatter began about what they were going to wear.

"Jeans," I said. "It's a wrap party, not a movie premiere. Don't get all confused and don't get your hopes up. This is really for the crew. You'll be lucky if the actors hang out, if they come at all."

Tess eyed me suspiciously.

"How do you know so much about the film industry all of a sudden?"

Just then, the bell over the door rang and our first customer of the day walked in. It was bright and early on Thursday morning and all hands were on deck from opening so we could hammer out all the details of the partnership. We'd just gotten through it when I brought up the wrap party. I knew it would derail the conversation and wisely kept it for the end.

"Hello, Mrs. Langley," I said, smiling at the familiar face of the seventy-year-old woman. I instinctively reached for a bag and began filling it with a chocolate danish.

"Good morning, Katie. Have you been out since the sun came up? It's absolutely glorious out there today. I think May is my favourite month of the year, despite the rain. Just watching those flowers bloom in the square across the street—"

"I know," I said, handing her the bag. "I

stop every morning to stare at those tulips. Makes me wish I knew how to paint. Just the sight of them in the long grass takes my breath away."

"Makes me thankful for small-town living. Bet city folk don't notice those things." She handed me a few bills and took the bag. Mrs. Langley never accepted change.

"I don't know. I think if you're the kind of person who appreciates something, you tend to do it wherever you are."

She shrugged, blew me a kiss, and walked out the door.

I spent the rest of the day serving the customers because Jax and Tess were far too distracted talking about *which* jeans and *which* shirts they should wear to the party. I was having second thoughts about having invited them. I'd wanted a security blanket with me, but they were causing me more anxiety than anything else. And we weren't even there yet.

Eventually, I shooed them both into the kitchen and put them to work so I didn't have to listen anymore. I was thankful for the constant stream of customers. My mind was also starting to wander.

*

I didn't hear from Mason all day Thursday, but he did text me Friday morning to give me the details for the party and make sure I was coming. When I told him I was, he texted back to say he was looking forward to seeing me. My belly did a little flip and I had to talk myself down, reminding myself this was the end, not the beginning.

The day dragged. If I'd thought Tess and Jax had been bad the day before, now it was even worse. They gossiped and speculated if Jessica would be there, if her fiancé would be there, and whether Max Irons, the supporting actor who'd won an Oscar the year before, would be there. By closing, I just wanted to scream.

"Want me to come over so we can get ready together?" Tess asked.

"No," I said, a little more harshly than I'd intended. "I mean, I just need to unwind a little. Why don't we share a cab over there? I'll call it and come pick you both up."

"That's a plan," Jax said. Tess nodded in agreement, trying to hide her disappointment. I felt bad, I did, but I needed time away from those two.

As we closed up the shop, we discussed the last details of the partnership agreement. We hadn't signed the papers yet, but we'd agreed on all the terms and the paperwork was being re-drawn. By next week, it would be a done deal. And even though Franni's might no longer be just mine, I couldn't help but think of the roads it opened up for me.

*

In the end, I opted for black leggings and a sleeveless white tunic top. I fished a pair of booties out of the back of my closet and stared at myself in the mirror. I was due for a cut and nothing I did would make my hair come alive. Frustrated, I pulled it up in a ponytail. I applied mascara and a little lipstick, and I was good to go.

As promised, I picked up Tess and Jax and opted to sit up front with the driver while they continued their incessant chatter. I made a mental note to ditch them as soon as we got there. I felt bad about it, but it had to be done.

We pulled up outside the venue, an old blues bar out by the old highway leading into town. It had been quiet lately, and I'd thought it had shut down, but Jax told me it had found new life as a gay bar. I never would've known it from the outside, but the moment I saw how great the inside looked, I believed him. Gone were the sawdust-covered floors and dirty table tops, in were the freshly painted chocolate-coloured walls and bistro-style seating.

There was a band playing and the place was packed. They'd rented out the entire bar for the party, and I was shocked to see how many people were involved in the making of a feature film. I recognized a few people from my short time on set, but my initial plan of ditching my safety net suddenly seemed iffy.

"There you are," Mason said, coming up beside me.

I turned to him and smiled, relieved to see a friendly face, elated it was his. He leaned in to kiss me and I must have made some serious eyes at him because he stopped at the last minute, glancing over at Tess and Jax. They didn't miss a thing.

"Hey, Tess. Jax. So glad you came. Please, circulate. I know Tess got the tour the other day, so she must know everyone by now. The food's great. Eat. I'm going to steal Katie for a minute."

And just like that, he took me by the elbow and guided me across the bar, towards the short hallway leading to the washrooms. He parked me by the wall and stood in front of me, grinning. I was just trying to breathe. The slight curl of his hair, the blue of his eyes, the whole movie star package. It was too much.

"What?" I asked.

"I may have changed my mind."

"About what?"

"Fucking you in the bathroom."

"What? No. We discussed this, Mason. That was a one-shot deal. You're leaving tomorrow."

"Sunday."

"Whatever. You know what I'm saying. The last thing I need is gossip. Most of your crew lives here, you know."

"I'd settle for a kiss."

We stared at each other for a moment.

"Is that a yes?" he asked hopefully.

I rolled my eyes.

"No. Do you not remember our conversation? It was two days ago."

"Fine. Forget it."

"Forgotten." I playfully punched him in the chest and then used the opportunity to slip away. I made my way back towards the bar with him in close pursuit.

"Friends?" he asked.

"Definitely friends."

"Let me buy you a drink."

"Aren't they free?" I asked.

"Technicality."

We walked over to the bar and I asked the bartender for a shot of Balvenie, neat. Mason looked at me, impressed.

"A Scotch drinker?"

"Not usually. But how often do I go to wrap parties?"

I looked around and sure enough, I spotted Jessica Thompson with who I assumed was her famous fiancé. There were a few other faces I knew from the big screen, but I couldn't put names to them. Just then, Jessica spotted us and came over.

"Is this her?" she asked Mason.

"This is her," he said.

Jessica turned to me and put out her hand.

"Hi, Katie, right? I'm Jessica. So nice to meet you."

I must have looked like I'd seen a ghost because Mason just burst out laughing.

"I thought you said you didn't get starstruck," he sputtered.

"I don't. But come on, this is just surreal." I took Jessica's hand. "Nice to meet you, too."

"You made the cake for Mark, the grip, right?"

Now it made sense.

"Yes. Did you like it?"

"Like it? I want you to do my wedding cake."

And I was struck dumb again.

"Katie?" Mason prompted.

"Yeah. Right. I mean, I'm flattered and

everything, but aren't you getting married in a couple of weeks? In Switzerland?"

"I am."

"Then, I'm not really sure how that's possible. . ."

"Well, I do. Mason tells me you cook. Turns out my personal on-set caterer had a last-minute emergency and can't follow us to Switzerland. If you want the job, it's yours. Of course, I'll pay extra for the cake. That's a separate contract."

"Um—"

"Hey! What's going on?" I turned to see Tess and Jax, who had just come up behind me. I had no idea how much they'd heard.

"Jessica just offered Katie a chance to come on location with us in Europe and work as her personal chef. And make her wedding cake," Mason offered. I could've killed him.

"What?" Jax yelled. "Oh my god. That's amazing."

"Don't get excited," I said. "I don't see how I can—"

"Of course she'll go," Tess interjected, turning to Jessica. "She'd love to go. I'm assuming you've got a special menu, correct? We'll get in touch with your management and get all the details."

"Tess!" I said.

"Katie," Mason said. "You just finished telling me you wanted to travel. You also told me you dream of making a name for yourself with your cakes. What more do you want? You think another opportunity like this is coming along tomorrow?"

I turned to Jax, hoping for a voice of reason, but he was just nodding his head like an idiot. Jessica was patiently waiting for an answer.

"Jax, we haven't even signed the papers yet." It was my last-ditch effort. "How can I leave you both for two weeks?"

"Easy," Jax said. "You just go. We got this."

Tess nodded and I shrugged, looking back at Jessica.

"I guess that's a yes."

She leaned over and hugged me.

"This is going to be great. You'll see. We leave Sunday. I'll have my manager call you tomorrow with all the details. I'll get your number from Mason."

And with that, she was gone. I stood there in shock, Tess and Jax grinning ear-to-fucking-ear while Mason looked at me with something suspiciously like pride in his expression.

"What?" I said.

He waited until Tess and Jax wandered away, replete with all new gossip to occupy themselves with. Then he turned to me.

"I'm just thinking about the possibilities. For us."

"Mason. There is no us. If I do this thing, nothing happens with us."

"You mean that."

"I do. Please. Don't make me say no to her."

"Why? Katie, we were amazing."

"We were. And if we got together again, it would be even more amazing. And then I'd fall for you. And we've already talked about all the reasons that wouldn't work."

"My life, your career."

"Exactly."

"Okay. Do me one favour, though?"

"What's that?"

"Dance with me."

CHAPTER SIXTEEN

My phone was ringing bright and early Saturday morning. I rolled over, about to shut it off when I remembered the previous night. I brought it to my ear, shutting my eyes against the light streaming through my window and cursing myself for having forgotten to close the blinds.

"Hello?" I said, breathless.

"Katie? Hi, this is Tina, Jessica's manager. I believe we have a few details to work out. I was wondering if we could schedule a call for say, 10 a.m.?"

I pulled the phone away to look at the time. Seven o'clock. Christ.

"Yeah. Sure. That would be great. We'll

speak then." I hung up the phone and placed it gently back down on the table.

Then I heard the toilet flush.

My eyes flew open as the rest of the night came roaring back. I lifted the sheets and peeked underneath. Naked. *Shit.* I pulled them up around me as Mason sauntered through the bedroom door, wearing nothing but boxer briefs and a shit-eating grin on his face.

"Good morning, beautiful."

"Oh, fuck."

He cocked his head from side to side a few times.

"Not the usual response, but I can live with it."

"What happened?"

He smiled and I wanted to throw my pillow across the room at him.

"Mason!"

"Fine, fine. Nothing happened. You got shit-faced at the party and I brought you home. I slept on the couch. You can check the blankets if you don't believe me."

Relief flooded through my body.

"Trust me," he continued. "If something had happened, you'd remember."

I blushed and pulled the sheets up tighter.

"You undressed me?" I asked, already knowing the answer.

"I've seen you naked before."

I nodded. True. And he had been a gentleman.

"Is there anything else I can do for you?" he asked, looking ever the mischievous imp.

"Breakfast?" I asked, hopeful.

He turned on his heel and left the room. Surprised, I fell back into bed for a moment and listened to the sounds of cabinet doors and pans moving around. I rolled out of bed and dug through my drawer for a T-shirt and sweats. Pulling them on, I went to join him in the kitchen.

Together, we made a decent breakfast of bacon, eggs, and pancakes. I even had some fresh fruit stashed in the bin in the fridge. We settled in at the table to eat. Thankfully, he'd put on some clothes before starting to cook.

"So was that Tina?" he asked.

"Yeah. She's calling back at ten to work out the details of the contract."

Mason nodded and took a sip of coffee. He made excellent coffee.

"This is going to be great for you, Katie. You'll see. There will be press, and people will talk about the cake. You never know where this will lead."

I smiled nervously, eager to change the subject.

"So did I make a fool of myself last night?"

"Absolutely not." Mason held up his hand, scout's honour. "You're actually a very cute drunk."

He paused, a funny look passing over his face.

"What? What did I do? Did I throw up?"

"No." He looked me in the eye. "You kissed me."

My hand flew to my mouth like we were in some kind of movie.

"Oh my god. Mason. You said nothing happened."

"Nothing did happen. I didn't let it."

"Why did I kiss you?"

"Well, according to you, it had been a long time since you'd last gotten laid, and apparently the other day had been really good for you—you went into it in some detail—and given that it was our last night together in Mountain Valley, and you hadn't signed any contract yet. . ."

"I did not say that."

"You did."

I swallowed. The truth was, as he spoke, I could see the whole scene playing out. I had said those things. Looking at him across the table, I realized I still wanted those things. The angel and devil did a furious battle over my

128

shoulder, each trying to plead their case in the thirty seconds I spent staring at him. Finally, I pushed them both aside and stood up.

I brought my dishes to the sink and heard his chair scrape the floor as he got up to follow suit. I stood there, hands on the counter, steadying myself until he came up behind me. I waited until he put his dishes down, then turned to him and put my hand on his cheek.

"It's been a really long time since I've gotten laid, and the other night was really good for me —"

Before I could say another word, his mouth was on mine. My body caught fire as his hands worked their way across my back, down to my ass, and then back up again. I snaked my hands up under his shirt, running them across the broad expanse of his back as he continued kissing me in that way that made me see stars. I pulled back.

"This is a mistake," I said.

"Do you want me to stop?"

"No."

"Then what do you want to do?"

Goddammit. Why did he have to be so *good*? If he'd been an asshole, I could've just kicked him out.

"I want to lay down some ground rules."

He didn't let go of me but gave me a quick

nod of the head. He was willing to listen.

"Once I step foot on the plane, nothing else happens."

He took in a sharp breath.

"So once again, you're telling me this is the last time?"

"This *is* the last time. Well, however many times we can squeeze in over the course of the day, providing you have no other plans?"

"Oh, I will cancel my plans. But I feel once we get on location, you're going to be telling me a different story."

"No, I won't."

"Oh, don't get me wrong. I'm fine with it. I just want you to understand you're the only one playing this game." He paused to pull my shirt up over my head. "Stop, start—" He ducked his head and swiped my nipple with his tongue. I gasped. "This is all you."

I had a rebuttal prepared, but I was beyond coherent speech at that point and rapidly losing my other faculties. His hand had slid down into the waistband of my sweats, cupping me. He leaned down and whispered in my ear.

"Have you ever fucked on your kitchen table, Katie Simon?"

I bit my lip and shook my head. In one quick motion, he pulled down my sweats as I stepped out of them. I reached for his pants and he stepped back, taking them off and tossing them aside. Then he grabbed me under the ass and lifted me up. I wrapped my legs around his waist, feeling his length against me and unable to resist the urge to rub against him. He groaned in my ear as he deposited me on the table.

"I am going to do things to you today that are going to make you blush every time you think about them," he whispered, leaving a trail of kisses from my ear to my lips. I leaned up to kiss him but he just skimmed my lips, working his way down my neck towards my chest. I sighed and rested my hands on the table behind me as I leaned back.

"I'm going to make you moan. I'm going to make you scream. I am going to make you come so many times you lose count."

By this time, he had his mouth around my breast, teasing my nipple with his tongue. I couldn't sit still, writhing on the table as his hands held my hips firmly. He ran his tongue down to my navel and I grabbed the back of his head with one hand before his face disappeared between my legs.

"Oh my fucking god," I cried.

"That's what I'm talking about," he murmured, the vibrations against my skin making me squirm with ecstasy.

He dropped to his knees and pulled me towards the edge of the table. Winding his arms underneath my knees, he spread my thighs wide and went to work. He traced every line, every curve of my most sensitive parts. He took his time, exploring, tasting, until I thought I was going mad.

"Please," I whimpered. He raised his head.

"Please, what?"

"Please. Make me come," I pleaded.

He smiled and dipped his head once more, closing his mouth around my clit and doing something with his tongue that drove me absolutely batshit insane. I looked down at him, watching him work me over, completely aroused by the sight of him between my legs. It was too much.

"Oh, god. Mason. Mason!"

I grabbed onto his hair with both hands, wrapping my legs around his neck as I came down from what was surely the most intense orgasm of my entire life. He rested his cheek on my thigh and I reached down to stroke his hair.

"I need a nap," I said.

He lifted his head and checked the clock on the counter.

"You've got a phone call in three minutes."

I followed his eyes to the clock and jumped

down off the table.

Holy shit.

*

An hour later, I was off the call and my head was spinning. Tina and I had hammered out all aspects of the deal and I had been inducted into the wonderful world of per diems. I was positively giddy. We had worked out separate contracts for the wedding and the location shoot, as promised, and I was shocked at how lucrative the whole package had turned out to be.

Naturally, Jessica was on a strict, no-carb pre-wedding diet and Tina sent me over a list of approved foods. Looking it over, I was once again glad I wasn't a celebrity. Despite the lack of variety, I would make her a delicious menu. Of that, I had no doubt. I was just hoping this wasn't her year-round diet.

I was lying on my stomach in bed, naked, scanning through the contract on my phone while Mason drew the letters of the alphabet on my back.

"Are you done yet?" he asked. "Can we continue?"

I set my phone aside and gave him my full attention.

"Talk to me," I said. He rolled his eyes.

"What do you want me to say? You already know pretty much everything."

"I doubt that. I got the Cliff Notes version of your past. What about your future? You have dreams of directing?"

He shrugged.

"I'd love to open a small production company. Produce indie films. Not in California. Somewhere quiet. Like here. It's such a great location. You must get so many movies shooting here."

"Some. We're more known for our music festival, actually. It's in late August and it's pretty famous across Canada."

"Even better. Untapped potential. Think of the tourist dollars for Franni's."

I stared at the ceiling as I thought about that for a moment. He wasn't wrong. With the lakes and mountains, we could double for a lot of US locations, in addition to some European ones.

"What's on your mind?" he asked.

"Mountains," I answered, without thinking.

He rolled onto his side and ran the tip of his finger along the slope of my breast.

"Funny. Me, too."

*

We spent the day in bed — talking, laughing, having sex. It was a perfect day, and I had zero regrets, until he started getting dressed to leave. I had to pack, he had to pack, and neither of us was getting anything done except each other.

I watched him pull on his pants and then he sat on the edge of the bed.

"I had fun today, Katie."

"So did I."

"Would you reconsider? Think how amazing it would be."

I sighed, then gathered all my inner strength to say what had to be said.

"It's amazing now because nobody knows. But if we're out there, on location, doing this? The press will be all over it. I don't want that. You yourself said you didn't want that for anyone."

"I said there's never been anyone worth trying for."

I paused, then got out of bed and pulled on some clothes. Anything to buy myself some time while I thought this through.

"We've known each other for seven seconds," I said.

"Long enough."

I motioned for him to get up, then guided him towards the front door. I wasn't having this conversation again. And I certainly wasn't having it now. We got to the door and I reached for the handle. He put out his hand to stop me.

"So you have nothing to say on the subject?"

"Nothing new," I agreed.

He stared at me, his expression completely indecipherable. Though that did nothing to stop my insides from melting.

"I like you, too," I conceded. "And I'm crazy thankful for this opportunity. And if things were different, if you weren't one of the most famous men in North America, well, who knows?"

"That's not fair," he interrupted.

"It's what it is." I opened the door. "We both agreed. Today was amazing. Better than amazing. Mind-blowing. Let's leave it at that, okay?"

"One last kiss?" he asked, leaning within inches of my lips. My heart skipped a couple of beats.

"It won't change anything," I whispered.

He pulled back and my heart dropped. *Shit.*

"All right, then," he said and walked out the door.

CHAPTER SEVENTEEN

At a little after nine o'clock that night, Tess and Jax came by to drive me to the airport. The flight left at one a.m., which seemed incredibly cruel but a relatively small price to pay for an all-expenses-paid trip to Switzerland. They were simultaneously drilling me with questions and giving me tons of advice. I was already exhausted from my emotionally and physically trying day, so dealing with those two wasn't high on my list of priorities.

I gave them both big hugs when they dropped me off at the departure gate. I went through security, picked up some emergency snacks, and boarded the plane. I was so tired I had no recollection of seeing any familiar faces in the departure lounge. I found my seat, closed my eyes, and crashed. I barely remember landing or changing planes, but at some point, I woke up in my new seat on the way to Zurich.

I turned and saw a woman, around 30, sitting next to me. She was flipping through the pages of a fashion magazine, sipping on a diet drink through a straw. I made a mental note to ask her how she got the full can. Glancing over and finding me awake, she put down the magazine and reached over to shake my hand.

"Katie, right? I'm Steph. I'm Mason's hair and makeup."

I sat up in my seat and rubbed my eyes before taking her hand and giving it a quick shake.

"So nice to meet you, Steph. I'm sorry I haven't been an ideal travel companion."

"Actually, you've been the best," she laughed.

We spent the rest of the flight getting to know each other. She had some amazing stories and filled me in on the cast and crew so I wouldn't feel so lost when we landed.

"Smell that?" she asked.

"Smell what?"

"Chicken. Must be chicken for dinner."

"Wow," I said. "You should work in the

kitchen."

"I have a very highly developed sense of smell, but I prefer hair and makeup, thank you very much. Though I hear Jessica's really great to work for. Her last chef was crushed not to come."

"How long have you been working for Mason?" I asked.

"This is our fourth film together. He's a dream. We've become close." She paused. "You two spent quite a bit of time together back in Canada, didn't you?"

"We did. I taught him how to bake his grandma's cinnamon buns." I laughed at the memory. "He's sweet. Not my type, though."

"Uh-huh." Steph picked up her magazine and flipped through a few pages. I figured the topic was dropped, but a few minutes later she muttered, "Just be careful."

*

We were shooting in a small mountain village called Grindelwald, about a two-hour drive from Zurich. The production had rented out an entire hotel for the cast and crew. It had a total Swiss-village vibe and I fell in love the moment I set foot into the lobby.

The two leads and the two supporting cast

occupied the top two floors, and the rest of the cast and crew were spread out through the rest of the hotel. The director had opted to take the caretaker's cottage outside, which looked like a beautiful little two-storey house.

I had the day to settle in while the department heads had a production meeting and met their local crew. The crew that traveled with us toured the locations and got oriented. I took the time to explore the hotel (spa!) and surrounding area, which was absolutely beautiful. I felt like I was in *The Sound of Music.* Wildflowers were everywhere. Once again, I wished I knew how to paint.

Sometime after lunch, just as I was contemplating an ill-advised nap, I bumped into Steph. She greeted me with a big smile and looped her arm through mine.

"I see that sleepy look in your eyes. Big mistake. Come with me," she said.

"Where are we going?" I asked.

She shrugged.

"Dunno. Never been here. Let's just walk around and stick our heads into the local shops. We'll find you the grocery stores you need for Jess."

I cursed myself for not even having thought of that.

We spent a great afternoon together. I had

been worried Steph would've had her fill of me on the plane, but she seemed to have taken me under her wing, which I really appreciated. She was married with two kids and an adorable dog that she kept showing me pictures of. I thought it a little odd that she had more pictures on her phone of her dog than her kids, but having neither myself, I kept my mouth shut.

In any case, she was a seasoned pro, and in no time we found everything I needed. I made a list to give to the production driver and Steph helped me find him when we got back to the hotel. Over the course of the day, I'd revealed to her my not-so-secret cake ambitions.

"This is a great opportunity for you," she said. "I'm sure it'll be the start of something amazing."

Her confidence in me was puzzling. We'd literally known each other less than a day. But it was exactly what I needed to hear at that moment, so I just took it as a gift.

*

After the initial excitement wore off, life on set turned out to be not so eventful. It helped that I wasn't Tess, prone to gush over every little thing I encountered, but in reality, there seemed to be nothing glamorous about the business at all. It was a lot of hurry up and wait. Everyone had to be in place, but then it took forever to get anything done.

Steph was glued to Mason's side whenever he wasn't in the middle of a take, so after lunch, I wandered around set until I stumbled upon a group of grips playing poker off in a far corner. After watching for a while, one of them asked if I wanted to join in. I sat down and let them deal me in.

About forty-five minutes later, there was a large pile of chips in front of me and a larger crowd around the table watching. I'd been deep in focus when I heard Mason's voice cut through the chatter.

"And what's going on over here?" he asked.

I looked up and our eyes met. It was the first time we'd seen each other since saying goodbye at my apartment. I'd seen him from a distance, of course, but he'd been working and we hadn't had a chance to talk. And there he was, mouth agape, staring at the poker table.

"Holy shit. Katie, are you beating Craig? No one beats Craig."

Craig, one of the gaffers who was sitting in on the game, sat up a little straighter but had a foul expression on his face. I hoped it wasn't too serious.

"Well, I've been beat today," Craig muttered.

Just then, the assistant director came over gave everyone their orders, so I sat at the table and counted out my winnings as the crew scattered. One of the production assistants was busy counting out the cash and the other players' chips, settling everyone up. Mason sat down in one of the empty seats.

"Don't you have to go?" I asked.

"It'll be a while before they're ready for me," he said. "How you getting along?"

I nodded and pointed my chin towards my winnings.

"Not too bad."

He laughed.

"Where'd you learn to play?"

"That college mistake? He was a pretty serious poker player. He took me to some underground games off-campus and taught me everything he knew," I said.

"So, a mistake that kinda paid off," he said. I laughed.

"I guess so. With a little distance, I guess so."

"Seriously. How's it going?"

"It's going great. I'm in Switzerland. In the Alps. I mean, come on. Jessica is great so far: likes everything I've fed her and barely eats anything anyway. I get to cook and hang out on a movie set."

"And stare at me all day."

I felt the blush creep into my cheeks and looked away.

"I'm staring at you, too," he whispered.

"Stop it."

He reached out his hand to take mine but I pulled it off the table, out of his reach.

"Walk me to my trailer," he said as he stood up. I reluctantly got up, took my money from the PA, and followed Mason off set. We'd been shooting inside and as soon as we walked out into the fresh air, it was like a whole new world. It was easy to forget where I was until I was standing on a mountaintop.

We walked over to his trailer, not saying a word. When we got there, he turned to me and brushed a loose strand of hair out of my face before I could stop him.

"We can't even be friends?" he asked.

I looked around. There was no one. I got up on my tiptoes and kissed him. He immediately reached out and wrapped one arm around my waist, drawing me closer. My head swam as I let have his way for a moment, and then I pulled back.

"No, we can't be friends."

I removed his arm from my waist and

walked away.

"That's not fair! I didn't know that was a test!" he called after me.

CHAPTER EIGHTEEN

It didn't take long to realize there wasn't much for me to do on set. Jessica ate when the cast ate, and she didn't put a morsel in her mouth at any other time. The wedding was scheduled for the weekend after the last shoot day. This was the last leg of the production, and she and her soon-to-be husband were planning a honeymoon on the French Riviera when it was done.

As a result, I'd be staying an extra three days after wrap. One afternoon during the first week, I sought out Stacie, Jessica's assistant, and asked her to introduce me to the caterers who were working the wedding. She had a driver bring me over there, and after that, I started spending afternoons in their kitchen. I took an inventory to make sure I had everything I'd need and made an order for ingredients. Despite Jess's extreme diet, or maybe because of it, she was going all-out on the wedding. Being in Switzerland, I was making a chocolate cake, and I was schoolgirl excited to get to work.

Jacques, the head chef, was a dream. Crusty on the outside, but a teddy bear underneath. Just like my Grandma Franni. He let me play around all week, experimenting with different chocolates and taste testing different recipes. It was so easy to work with him I found myself fantasizing about joining his kitchen staff—until I remembered I had my own kitchen back home.

Jessica's fiancé, who I finally learned was a director named Dean Johnson, was currently on his own shoot and was only flying into Zurich a day before the wedding. Most of the Hollywood A-List was due to show, and I'd heard rumours a few planes had been chartered for the occasion.

Part of the reason I spent so much time off set was Mason. Whenever I was near him, I couldn't think straight. All I could think about were his hands on my body, his tongue delving into my deepest parts, making me feel things

I'd never felt before. I'd be standing there, watching him run through a scene, and realize my breathing had completely changed and my panties were damp. It wasn't sustainable.

The weekend was only a day away. We had two days off sandwiched between two 14-hour-a-day, 5-day weeks. Apparently, if they were home, the crew would use that time to catch up on rest and laundry, but since they were here, everyone was planning day trips around the country, some even going overnight to Austria or Italy. I decided to stay put, having never been to Switzerland. I didn't want to get greedy. There was plenty in the area to explore.

"You sure?" Steph asked. "It's Florence. It's like, 6 hours by train. We're taking an overnight and we'll have a day to shop."

"I'm positive. Thanks for the invite. But I'm going to stay here. I've got the wedding to prep for, and I'm kind of in love with the Alps."

"Suit yourself," she said. "I'll bring you a souvenir."

"Deal."

We were in her hotel room and she was packing up for her trip. We had a few minutes left before we had to leave for set and she'd asked me if I wanted to walk over with her. I assumed it was just to invite me with her for the weekend, but as we approached set, she cleared her throat in a way that made it clear she had something to say.

"What's up?" I asked, stopping before we reached the PA at the gate.

"Well, I was just wondering, and you don't have to tell me, but is anything going on with you and Mason?"

"No. Nothing."

"Oh."

I sighed.

"What makes you ask?"

"Well, as I said, this isn't my first rodeo with him, and he just seems. . .different somehow. Not necessarily distracted, but like, for the first time, the role isn't the only thing on his mind. And the only variable here is you, and I know you're friends, so I thought perhaps—"

"You thought wrong. I'm sorry."

"Understood. But just so you know, he's a great guy. A really great guy. I've worked for a lot of assholes, and he's not one. Despite the fame, he's down-to-earth. I mean, he's got an ego, but how could you not in that position? And I know I kinda warned you away earlier, but that was before I knew you. All I'm saying is, if there is the slightest possibility? Maybe give it a chance."

I smiled tightly and indicated she should lead the way on set. She gave me a curt nod, indicating she understood completely. The subject was closed.

*

Saturday morning, I woke up late and stretched out in bed, staring out the window at a view I would never tire of. One large bird flew in a low circular pattern over the tallest peak and I watched as it dove for prey. I rolled over and looked at my phone. It was past ten. I hadn't slept past six all week. The jetlag had never really worn off and the extra sleep had done me a world of good.

I got up and headed for the bathroom. After a quick shower, I dressed, figuring I'd head out for something to eat. Before bed, I'd planned out a hike for myself and I was eager to get going. But not before coffee.

I stepped out of my room and headed for the staircase. I stopped short when I saw Mason coming down the stairs. He stopped, too, and for a comical moment, we just stood there staring at each other, mouths agape.

"What are you doing here?" he asked.

"I was going to get breakfast. What are you doing here?"

"Same."

"I mean, why did you stay? Everyone else

took off."

He shrugged.

"I'm not everyone else."

I just stood there, unsure of what to do next. I wanted to ask him to join me, but I didn't want to send mixed signals. And being around him mixed my own signals, so—

"Hey. I had a day trip planned today. Come with me," he said.

"I'd love to, but I've got one of my own."

"I bet mine's better."

"Doubt it."

"Does yours involve a postal bus?"

I stared at him, dumbfounded.

"No, I can't say it does."

"Go back to your room and grab a sweater. I'll wait."

"I didn't say I was going with you."

"Please come with me."

My heart did not want to say no. I cursed myself for being so weak, but at the same time, I was in complete control. If I didn't want anything to happen, nothing was going to happen. I just had to keep my distance.

"Wait here," I said.

CHAPTER NINETEEN

We got off the train in Lauterbrunnen and I was instantly charmed by the even smaller-town feel that I'd experienced in Grindelwald. Mason had been very tight-lipped on the twenty-minute train ride and I was burning with curiosity.

"Where are we going?" I asked for the thousandth time that morning.

"You'll see," he answered for the thousandth time. "Actually. For a kiss, I'll tell you."

I slapped his chest and instantly regretted it. The spark I felt echo through my body was enough to remind me how close to the edge we were treading. And even in a tiny town like this, there was no way to be certain paparazzi wasn't lurking.

He was back in his baseball hat and shades because he'd insisted he didn't want anyone from production coming with us as security. I was also back to calling him Mark again, which felt weird after everything that had happened between us. But the set had been swarmed with press since the shoot began. Between the film, the cast, and the upcoming wedding, it was the talk of the town. Of every town. It wasn't worth the risk.

"I'll live with the suspense," I said.

He put his hand on the small of my back and led me down a small road towards a bus. The only bus. It was just waiting there. I looked at him.

"Postal bus." He nodded, pleased I'd remembered.

We boarded the bus and found a seat. More passengers trickled on and after a few minutes, the driver started the engine. Ten minutes later, he deposited us at the base of a gondola station. I looked up, following the cable up to an impossible height. I turned to Mason, and from the look in his eyes, I knew I wore the expression of childlike glee. It was certainly what I was feeling.

"Oh my god. We're going up there?" I asked.

"We're going up there."

He reached for my hand and without thinking, I let him take it. I registered the flood of heat coursing through my veins at his touch, but I held on, fueled by excitement at what lay ahead. We got off the bus and I was practically vibrating. I loved the mountains—it was the main perk of living at home. But this was on a completely different scale, and to think we were going *up there*. Possibly even hiking up there.

"Are we going hiking up there?" I asked.

"Yes, Ma'am."

I could've kissed him. I wanted to kiss him. I looked down when I remembered we were holding hands, and I smiled to myself. It was enough. He must've known what I was thinking because at that moment he gave my hand a squeeze.

"I'm not going to start again, I promise. Let's just go up and have a great day," he said.

*

The gondola ride was magic. I felt like I was ascending into the heavens. I couldn't look down, even though Mason kept trying to convince me, but I kept my eye on our destination ahead and that was more than enough for me. He held my hand the entire way up, and I'd be surprised if I hadn't cut off his blood supply. Despite the beauty, there was a definite degree of fear at play.

When we got off the gondola, we both just stopped and looked around in wonder.

"Have you ever been here before?" I asked. He shook his head slowly.

"Never. But friends who backpacked across Europe told me about it and I figured since I was so close, it would be a shame not to come."

"Thank you for bringing me."

He turned to look at me and lifted my chin with his finger so I had no choice but to make eye contact.

"I'm so glad you're here."

We stared at each other for a moment, the air charged between us, but then he broke the spell by dropping his hand and walking towards the cluster of buildings that seemed to make up the town. I took another last look at the gondola before following him, quickening my step until we were side by side once again.

"Rumour has it they wanted to turn this into a ski resort, but they managed to avoid it due to some zoning regulation or something," Mason said.

"I imagine it would've looked very different if that had happened."

The area looked like it was untouched by outside life. There were absolutely no cars or vehicles of any kind. The only way in or out was by foot or gondola. There was a scattering of Swiss-style buildings—some restaurants, a hotel, a hostel, and a couple of shops and residences.

Mason pulled a map out of his pocket and I laughed. I hadn't seen a paper map in ages.

"Don't laugh," he said. "You'll be happy we have this. Put on your sweater."

And with that, he led me off down a trail that wound through some mountains, and before I knew it, we were hiking among giant sheets of ice. Our heads were literally in the clouds. It was the most amazing thing I'd ever experienced.

"Mason, this is…unreal. I can't believe we're even here." I reached out, my hand passing through the vapour.

He flashed me a smile and indicated I should follow him.

"You ain't seen nothing yet."

"Can we stop for a second?"

"Yeah. Sure thing."

He pulled off his sweatshirt, dislodging the baseball cap at the same time. He looked at it, but let it sit on the ground as he spread out his shirt for me to sit on. Once I was settled, he sat beside me, reaching over for his cap and rubbing off the splashes of water and mud. Then he reached into his backpack and pulled out a bottle of water, which he opened and handed to me. I took a grateful sip and passed it back.

"Thank you," I said. He nodded and took a swig before putting the bottle back in his bag.

"I never get the chance to do shit like this," he said.

"Why not? You're a movie star. You should do whatever you want."

"I'm only a movie star so long as I'm working. And when you work as much as I do, it doesn't leave much time for things like this."

"Kind of makes you stop and think about what's important, doesn't it?" I asked.

"It does. But by the same token, without the work, I likely couldn't afford to even be here."

"Don't say that," I said. "You might luck out and get a catering job like I did."

He laughed and I smiled, pleased that I'd amused him.

"It's not fair, you know," I said.

"What isn't?"

"You didn't tell me you were taking me to the most romantic spot on earth."

He looked at me, amazed.

"You are unlike any woman I've ever met,

Katie Simon."

"Why? You're telling me this isn't romantic?"

"I think it is. Most women would think we're sitting in a pile of mud on the side of a mountain."

"Well, we are. But it's Swiss mud. And it's the freaking Alps."

With that, Mason laughed and stood up, reaching down to help me up as well. I took his hand and we walked slowly back towards the path. We continued in silence for a while, both of us lost in our thoughts. I was trying to understand how I could feel so close to someone I'd known for so little time, especially someone like him. If anyone had told me a month ago I'd be standing on top of the Swiss Alps with one of the most famous actors in the world, I'd have told them they were nuts. Yet there I was.

"Katie. Look."

I looked up and saw the most incredible waterfall directly in front of us. It was coming off a tall cliff, just a narrow stream of water flowing over the ice that had frozen on its way down. It was understated in the traditional sense of a waterfall, but the fact that it just kept going, despite freezing over time and time again, was something spectacular to behold.

We both stood there, silent. I reached for his hand and he took it, neither of us taking our eyes off the miracle in front of us. It felt like we were sharing a moment, something that would stay with us forever. I have no idea how long we were there, standing in a puddle of ice and mud, heads literally in the clouds.

CHAPTER TWENTY

"Let's stay the night," Mason said.

We'd just finished eating dinner at the hotel restaurant and we were both exhausted from the afternoon. I turned the idea over in my mind, weighing the pros and cons, and eventually deciding I only lived once, so—

"Sure. But we've got to get back first thing in the morning. I promised Chef Jacques I'd be in the kitchen."

"Scout's honour."

"Were you ever a Scout?" I asked playfully. He cocked his head and winked.

"I played one on TV."

I laughed just as the waiter came by to take our dessert orders. Mason ordered everything chocolate on the menu, which I couldn't argue with.

"Stay here," he said, standing up. "I'll go take care of the reservation."

I watched him walk through the small restaurant and disappear towards the reception desk. In his absence, the waiter appeared with the array of desserts and I wasted no time picking up my fork and digging in. I was halfway through a chocolate souffle when Mason returned, and I looked up with what was surely a guilty expression on my face.

"Professional interest," I said.

He rolled his eyes and sat down. He said nothing as he grabbed his fork and tried to catch up. The coffee was amazing, and the combination of the chocolate and coffee together? Oh my god.

"You're quiet," I said.

"Nothing much to say, is there? Now shush and let me eat, woman."

*

By the time we polished off every pastry, cake, and all the ice cream, neither of us could move. We ordered a couple of nightcaps in the hope of staving off the effects of the caffeine and by the time we were done, we were both pleasantly tipsy. I could tell he was feeling it by the shine in his eyes. And the way he staggered a little when he got up from the table.

"Upstairs?" I asked. He nodded and I followed him to the staircase. When we got to the second floor, he pointed left and we both walked the corridor, still relatively silent. I didn't know what was on his mind, but I wondered whether he'd booked one room or two. Part of me was hoping it was one.

"Here you go," he said, passing me the key. I swallowed and smiled.

"Where are you?" I asked.

"Just across the way." He indicated the door behind him.

I took the key from him and let myself in. It was a cute little room, sparsely decorated but very comfortable looking. I glanced at the bed and felt the blush creep up my cheeks. Mason cleared his throat behind me. He'd followed me in.

"So, uh, have a good night?" he said. I nodded.

"You, too. You'll have to excuse me in advance for how I'm going to look in the morning. Wasn't really planning on an overnighter."

He reached out and touched my cheek.

"You're always beautiful," he said. Then he

walked out of the room and gently closed the door.

I sat on the edge of the bed and stared at the door, thinking maybe if I tried hard enough I'd develop x-ray vision. He hadn't even attempted a kiss. Although he'd promised me he wouldn't. But after such an incredibly romantic day, I couldn't believe he'd hold off if he'd really wanted to.

I was confused. I didn't want to go after him and send him mixed signals. I still had no interest in being in the spotlight. He was right. Our relationship could never withstand that. We just didn't know each other well enough yet. But on the other hand, well—

I figured I'd make a list. I searched through the drawers until I found a hotel notepad and pencil, drew a line down the centre, and wrote "pros" and "cons" on either side. Just as I was about to start writing, there was a knock at the door. I jumped up, crossed the room, and opened it. There he was.

"I just meant to ask you—"

Fuck it.

I put my finger to his lips, got up on my tiptoes, and kissed him. I pulled back and eyed him tentatively. He was smiling, so I kissed him again. That was all he needed. He walked me into the room and shut the door, never breaking the kiss. I unzipped his hoodie and pushed it off his shoulders, anxious to get my hands on his bare skin. I felt like I'd been starving myself for weeks and there was this feast laid out in front of me, if only I could get to it.

He broke away to pull off his shirt and I took the opportunity to strip out of all my clothes. He laughed.

"In a rush, are you?"

I stopped.

"Listen, this doesn't mean—"

"I know exactly what it means, don't worry." He undid his pants and stepped out of them before approaching me again, and I took the millisecond I had to appreciate the cut of his muscle and the firmness of his abs. A feast indeed.

He gathered me up in his arms and found my mouth with his. I melted against him, exhaustion from the day combining with rising passion. I wound my arms around his waist, holding him close. He walked us over to the bed and we lay down, side by side, and gazed into each other's eyes.

"I meant it; you are beautiful."

"I don't care about beauty. Tell me something else."

"You're strong. Driven. Smart. Sexy."

As he continued his list, I climbed on top of him and leaned over, silencing him with my mouth. He held the back of my head as he kissed me, a move that always sent chills down my spine. I started moving against him and felt him grow hard beneath me. I shifted, kissing my way in a line down his neck, across his chest, taking my time to swirl my tongue around each of his perfectly erect nipples. He groaned beneath me, the sound bolstering my confidence as I continued downward.

"Katie—"

"Hmmm."

I traced a path across his abdomen with my tongue, watching the gooseflesh crop up in its wake. It was heady, having such a visible effect on him. None more visible than what was going on below his waist. I took him in my hand and he groaned again, whispering my name. I rose up on my knees and dipped my head, taking him in my mouth slowly, seeing how far I could take him in. Judging by the sounds he was making, I'd say just enough.

"Oh, God, Katie. No—"

I knew what he was thinking. I also knew we were young and fit and he at least another round in him before morning came. For all the pleasure he'd shown me, it was payback time. I ran my tongue up the underside of his shaft, pressing firmly on the vein that led to the tip.

"Oh, fuck—"

I smiled to myself, wondering which was the greater compliment - God or fuck? Either way, I was getting more and more turned on as I worked him over. After teasing him with my tongue, I could feel my hips moving, grinding against the air. I took him in my mouth again, wrapping one hand firmly around the base, allowing me greater control.

His hand slid up my leg towards the apex of my thighs. I pushed into his hand and his finger slid easily inside, finding my G-spot and massaging lightly. I moaned around his cock, causing him to swell even further in my mouth. His thumb found my clit as I continued to suck, and we worked together in rhythm, both of us drawing closer and closer until finally I sailed over the edge, coming with a fierce intensity while he was still in my mouth.

"Fuck, Katie, that is so hot."

He grabbed my head with his free hand, winding his fingers through my hair, and I felt his hips jerks as he came. I waited until he was done, cleaning him off with my tongue before lying down and resting my head on his thigh.

"Jesus Christ," he said. "Where you been hiding that skill?"

After a very long night that didn't involve very much sleep, we cleaned up as best as we could and made our way back to Grindelwald. When we arrived at the train station, I had Mason call his driver while I walked back to the hotel. I wasn't taking any chances.

As I walked, I thought about my situation. Despite what I'd told him, there was no way Mason and I would be able to keep our hands off each other for the rest of the week. Or at least, given the chance, I knew I wouldn't. I also knew there was no future for us.

But in exactly eight days, I'd be boarding a plane home and I'd probably never see him again. I was fooling myself, thinking I could play this game without getting hurt. I'd only ever had two real relationships, and it was likely what was going on with us was pure chemistry. It couldn't be anything else. And chances were good that by the end of the week, we'd be bored with each other.

Or at least that's what I told myself as I walked into the hotel and saw him standing at reception, talking to Steph. I smiled as I approached.

"Hey. How are you two doing? Good weekend?"

"Amazing," Steph said. "You?"

"Quiet. But nice. What about you, Mason?"

"Also quiet, but I did a bit of touring. Saw some interesting sights."

I cleared my throat and turned to the woman behind the desk in an attempt to hide my face, which I knew must be crimson. When the hell did I start blushing? The woman, late 60s, white-haired and dressed in what can only be described as a frock, smiled politely at me.

"Yes? May I help you?" she asked.

"Yes, please. I seem to have misplaced my key. I was wondering if you had a spare?"

"Not a problem, dear." She turned behind her towards a pegboard marked with room numbers and keys and took down a spare, handing it to me across the counter.

"Thank you," I said.

I smiled at the three of them then headed for the stairs.

"Wait up, I'll walk you," Mason said.

I paused, silently cursing him. When he caught up to me, we walked to the staircase, silent until we were sure we were out of earshot.

"What are you doing?" I asked.

"When did you lose your key?" he asked, ignoring my question altogether.

I smiled wickedly and extracted the key from

my pocket, discreetly slipping it into his hand.

"I didn't."

He stared at me in shock as I walked away.

CHAPTER TWENTY-ONE

I spent the afternoon with Chef Jacques as planned, going over my list and checking everything twice. This was my big shot and I wasn't going to screw it up. At one point, he brought over the menu he had planned for the wedding and asked my opinion. I didn't know if I was more shocked or honoured.

"Everything looks amazing, Chef. Did you think of adding duxelle to the second appetizer?"

His eyes widened as he considered the suggestion.

"That's an excellent idea, Katie. Maybe you should have been a chef instead of a baker."

I laughed.

"I do enjoy cooking, but baking is where my heart is."

"I can tell. You said your grandmother taught you?"

"She did." I got to work cleaning up my station. "She was very patient with me, starting from a very young age. By the time I was ten, I could bake almost anything decently. Didn't really master souffles until I hit 12 or 13."

Jacques laughed.

"Seriously, though. Most of my best memories are from those days, working side by side with her in the kitchen. Rolling out dough, kneading bread. She expressed her love through baking and I think she passed that on to me. It's why I could never consider selling my bakery."

He nodded solemnly in complete understanding, and we went about our business in silence.

*

I stopped on the walk back to the hotel to grab something to eat. There weren't many options, but that was fine with me. I was exhausted after the weekend and looking forward to crawling into bed and passing out. We had an early call the next morning and I desperately needed sleep.

Nevertheless, I took my time walking back. I only had another week and I wanted to savour the scenery—the peaks of the Alps and the dips of the valleys. I'd fallen in love with the Swiss architecture and the whole feel of the little mountain town, so different from my own.

I inserted the key in the lock and turned the handle of the door, but when I walked in, I found Mason lying on my bed, Cheshire-Cat grin on his face.

"Where the hell have you been?" he asked.

I put down my bag and kicked off my shoes, slowly making my way towards him.

"In the kitchen. And I'm wiped. But seeing you here may be bringing on a second wind."

I returned his sly smile as I crawled onto the bed beside him and reached for his belt, but he put out his hand to stop me.

"What's up?" I asked.

He lifted his hand to run his finger down my jawline, then trailed a path down my neck towards my breasts.

"I want to watch you," he said.

I raised my eyebrows, skeptical.

"Excuse me?"

"You heard me."

"Mason—"

"Katie."

"I can't. I mean—"

"Hear me out. The first time we had sex, you told me you were the sweet, in-the-dark, under-the-covers type. You've been anything but. We don't have a lot of time left together. Let's do some of those other things you've never done before."

He rolled off the bed, leaned over, and turned on the bedside lamp. Then he crossed the room to turn off the overhead lights.

"Stand up," he said.

Without thinking, I stood.

"Take off your clothes."

This time I hesitated.

"Katie. I've seen you naked. Just take off your clothes for me."

I slowly disrobed, incredibly conscious of him watching me but refusing to let that stop me. He *had* seen me naked. In much brighter light than this. When I was done, I looked up to find him gazing at me, the soft expression on his face darkening into something more like need.

"Now what?" I asked.

"Lie down."

I got onto the bed and lay down, propping my head up on the pillows against the headboard. I was a little shy, but it was nowhere near as bad as I thought it would be.

This was suddenly seeming doable. And more than a little hot, judging by the warmth spreading between my legs.

"I just want you to run your hand along your breast, just lightly."

I did as asked, watching my nipples rise up in response. I squeezed my thighs together, already wet.

"You can close your eyes if you're shy, but it's much hotter when you look at me."

I raised my eyes to meet his, which were now hooded with lust. My breathing deepened as I traced a line with my finger down towards my belly, flattening my palm as I reached between my thighs.

"Is that so bad?" he asked, his voice thick.

I shook my head.

"I want to look at you. Take off your clothes," I said.

Mason stripped down immediately, and when he stood, I could see how hard he was. I slipped a finger inside myself, past the slick flesh that would settle for me, but really wanted him. I moaned softly, spreading my thighs apart as he wrapped his hand around himself.

"You're already hard."

"It's all you. Just watching you. How does that make you feel?"

"Damn sexy."

"Good," he growled.

I moaned again, sliding down on the bed, momentarily forgetting about him as I got lost in the sensations taking over my body. I bent my knees, raising my hips to thrust into my hand, my palm rubbing against my clit in a way that was going to send me over the edge. I heard him groan, then rummage around before I heard the rip of the foil. The next thing I knew, he was lowering himself on top of me, removing my hand and replacing it with his hard length.

"Oh, yes, Mason. Yes."

We moved together, slowly at first, and then building up a steady rhythm that grew until I cried out, my fingernails digging into his flesh as I wrapped my legs around his waist. But he wasn't done. He unwrapped my legs, grabbed my ankles, and brought them up over his shoulders, penetrating so deep I could feel a second orgasm building. I reached down between us to where our bodies were joined and rubbed my clit against him as he moved in and out. He looked down, watching, and it was enough to do him in.

"Fuck, Katie," he cried as we both came together.

He collapsed on top of me, covering my neck

in tiny kisses. I wrapped my arms around him, pulling him in as close as I could, never wanting to let him go.

CHAPTER TWENTY-TWO

The week flew by. I spent Monday dividing my time between set and Chef Jacques' kitchen, and by the end of the day, I decided to prepare all of Jessica's meals in the latter. I told myself it was for convenience—Chef definitely had a better-equipped kitchen than the set—but that wasn't the case. I couldn't figure out how to be around Mason every day while pretending there was nothing going on between us. I wanted to brush the hair out of his eye, run my hand along his bicep. It was an impossible situation.

So I worked off-set. I had drivers come and collect the meals and every night when I returned to the hotel, I'd wait for Mason to finish his day. He would inevitably show up sometime around ten, and we'd waste no time shedding our clothes and getting to work. He was intent on having me try something new every day. I raised no objections.

On Sunday night, he'd brought a box of condoms into my room. By Thursday, he'd had to replace them. Given he was working fourteen-hour days, it was pretty damn impressive.

"What's on your mind?" he asked one night as we were lying in bed, tangled up in each other.

"Would you believe me if I said chocolate ganache?"

He shook his head and leaned over to kiss my forehead.

"Try again," he said.

"I'm thinking I never knew sex was supposed to be like this."

That got a smile.

"I mean, I always thought I'd had good sex before, but this has been different. I feel so much freer with you. You make me feel—"

"Sexy?"

"Yes."

"Because you are."

I smiled and turned my head. He reached over and took my chin, gently guiding my gaze back towards him.

"Hey. We've only got a few more nights. Lots more things I want to try."

He kissed me gently on the mouth and I parted my lips, offering him more. He growled low in his throat and moved towards me just as we heard a knock at the door. I flew up and checked the time. It was 11:30.

"Yes?" I called.

"Katie? It's me," Steph answered. "Can I come in for a minute?"

"Uh, yeah, sure, hold on. Let me throw on some clothes."

I pushed Mason out of the bed and directed him to the bathroom. He looked at me in disbelief. He opened his mouth in protest, but I silently shushed him. He reluctantly let me steer him into the bathroom and after I threw his clothes in behind him, I quietly closed the door. Then I let Steph in.

"Hey. What's up?" I asked.

"Well, the wedding is in a couple of days. I just wanted to make sure you were good, had everything you needed."

"Yeah, I'm great. Thanks."

"Do you want me to do your hair and makeup? I thought it might be fun."

"Oh," I said, surprised. "That's really nice of you, but I don't think it's necessary. I'll be in the kitchen all night."

"Uh, no you won't."

"What?"

"Yeah. Jess showed me the seating chart tonight. We're at the same table."

"WHAT?"

Steph just nodded.

"I'm not surprised. So like her. Does this mean—?"

"That I don't have a dress? Yes. That's exactly what this means. And I'm not going in a dirndl."

Steph laughed.

"Don't be ridiculous. Break away from that kitchen you've been hiding in and meet me on set tomorrow. I've got an idea."

"Sure," I said. "That would be great. Thank you."

"My pleasure." Steph turned towards the door. "Have a great night."

"You, too."

"Yeah. You, too, Mason. Don't forget you've got an early call tomorrow."

I stared at her, mouth wide open. She just opened the door and walked out. I could hear Mason laughing in the bathroom.

I threw open the door and found him standing there, still stark naked, doubled over with laughter.

"How did she know? Did you tell her?"

He shook his head, the laughter finally fading.

"No." He wiped a tear from his eye. "The first night we both came back from Grindelwald. That woman has an uncanny sense of smell. She said we smelled exactly the same. There was no point denying it. She knows everything about me. Don't worry. She's a vault."

I sighed and sat on the bed. Mason walked over and got on his knees before me.

"Now, where were we?" he asked.

*

Friday was the last day of shooting on the film. Three locations over two months and the cast and crew were exhausted. I showed up after lunch and Steph immediately grabbed my elbow and led me towards the wardrobe department. Connie, the costume designer, was already waiting with a selection of dresses.

"So? Which do you think?" Steph asked.

"Really? Well—" I started.

"I wasn't asking you. I was asking Connie. I don't trust your judgment one bit when it comes to yourself."

Connie looked me up and down and then

surveyed the dresses she'd chosen. She pulled out a green one with a plunging neckline and flowing skirt. It was stunning.

"This one will be perfect for you. And Jess didn't even end up wearing it in the film. No one's seen it. You will look spectacular."

"Are you sure?" I asked. I was overcome by the generosity of someone I didn't even know two weeks earlier.

"Positive. As a matter of fact, why don't you keep it? Give me ten bucks and I'll say I sold it to you during the post-production wardrobe sale."

I reached into my pocket and grabbed a twenty.

"Keep the change," I laughed.

"Go try it on."

I took the dress and got behind one of the curtains. It was almost a perfect fit; just a few small adjustments needed to be made. I never realized Jessica and I shared a body type. Funny. I considered her to be on another level. But there I was, rocking her dress.

I stepped out from behind the curtain and both women smiled uncontrollably.

"Hold on, let me get some pins," Connie said, rifling around in one of her cases.

She then proceeded to pin and tuck and chalk while I stood still and waited patiently. I could see her working in the mirror, but I couldn't take my eyes off myself. I looked gorgeous.

CHAPTER TWENTY-THREE

That night, I went back to my room alone to rest up for the wedding the next day. Since Jessica had invited the entire cast and crew, there was no wrap party. Regardless, Mason was down in the hotel bar drinking with Jessica, her fiancé Dean, and a few other members of the cast. He'd invited me, and I'd flatly refused.

I had just taken a shower and was lying in bed reading a book when I heard the gentle knock on my door.

"Katie? You up?"

It was Steph, and I got up to let her in. She was carrying a garment bag and a smile broke out on my face.

"Is that the dress?" I asked.

"Yup. Let's see it." She unzipped the bag and pulled it off the hanger while I pulled off my robe. Clad in just my underwear, I stepped into the dress and she helped me with the zipper. Then I turned and looked in the mirror. It was absolutely breathtaking.

"Wow," I said.

"Wow," Steph repeated.

"Shoes," I said.

"Got you covered." She reached into the bottom of the garment bag and pulled out a pair of nude heels. Just my size. I slid them on and they fit perfectly. Comfortable, even.

"Take off the dress," Steph said.

Without questioning her, I took it off and put it back on the hanger. As I pulled my robe back on, she pointed to the chair by the desk.

"Sit."

I sat. Steph reached for her giant purse, which she'd put on the bed a few minutes earlier, and pulled out her comb and a pair of scissors.

"Oh," I said.

"Yup."

She walked over and pulled the towel off my head. Then she started combing it through.

"Look, I appreciate it, I really do, but it's pointless. There is nothing you can do to bring this hair to life."

"Well," Steph said. "That's just insulting."

"Oh! No! I didn't mean—"

"It's okay. I'm kidding," she laughed. "But trust me. I know a thing or two about this."

I smiled at her, then turned to face forward. I was a little unnerved that there was no mirror. I'd have preferred to watch, but the moment I heard that first snip of the scissors, I decided I was better off this way.

Fifteen minutes later, Steph stood back and appraised me. Smiling, she leaned in and cut a few more snips here and there. I reached up to touch my head and she slapped my hand away. She went back to the bed, pulled a hairdryer out of her bag, and plugged it in.

"You don't look until I'm done," she said.

*

After Steph left, I stood in front of the bathroom mirror staring at my reflection in utter disbelief. I was beautiful. No, I was stunning. Maybe even gorgeous. She'd left my hair shoulder length, but had given it so many layers that it actually had body. It moved when I moved. It framed my face. It did all the things hair normally did on other people. Now it was doing it on me.

I heard another knock at the door and figured she must've forgotten something. As I got closer, I heard Mason on the other side fidgeting with his key. I sped up and put the weight of my body against the door.

"What's up?" he asked through the door, sounding more than a little tipsy.

"Not tonight, Mason. You're making a scene. Go upstairs."

He grumbled a little under his breath and eventually left. I smiled in relief. The dress? The hair? I wanted the whole picture to be a surprise.

I turned off the light, slipped off the robe, and crawled back into bed. It may have been Jessica's wedding, but I was the one with the biggest day of my life ahead of me.

CHAPTER TWENTY-FOUR

The day of the wedding, Chef Jacques dismissed me from the kitchen at around three o'clock, saying he would have his staff take care of everything from that point on. I'd done everything I could. I took a final, loving look at the cake that was about to transform my life and at the last moment, snapped a picture. Then I went back to the hotel and, with Steph's help, got ready for the wedding.

I'd managed to avoid Mason the entire day. He texted a few times and I deflected, telling him I was busy. By that point, there was no way I could prevent him from wanting to spend time with me at the reception. The cast and crew knew we were friends, but aside from

Steph, I didn't think anyone else knew what was going on. But this was essentially our last night together and we were going to be at a wedding. No matter what I told myself, the outcome was inevitable.

We'd come to an understanding over the course of the week, one I think we were both comfortable with. What was happening between us was amazing, but necessarily short-lived. We agreed not to have any hard feelings when it ended, and to stay in touch. I had no illusions about the feasibility of that, given his crazy schedule, but it was something he'd insisted on. And if I was being honest with myself, I wasn't opposed to the idea. If he should pass through town again, and I was still single. . .wild horses couldn't keep me away.

Mason had given me a gift. He had showered me with friendship and romance with no strings attached. He showed me what sex could be like. He taught me how to ask for what I wanted. The things we'd done over the past week, I never would've imagined possible mere months ago. I hadn't known my body was capable of pleasure like that. As I slipped into my dress, I vowed to spend the night thanking him.

"Wow." Steph let out a low whistle as the fabric settled around my body. I couldn't help but smile. "Katie. You look. I don't know. I mean. Shit, girl."

I laughed and looked at myself in the mirror. My hair was perfect. Steph had worked miracles bringing it to life and it framed my face perfectly. She'd also done my makeup so well it looked like I wasn't wearing any. And then the dress. I had to admit I looked fabulous. I slid my feet into the shoes and twirled around, watching the skirt fan out around me.

"I feel like a movie star," I said.

"You look like one."

With that, we headed off to the venue.

*

It was spectacular. There was no other way to describe it. The entire affair was set up outdoors in a large open area nestled between the mountains. There were separate open-air tents for dining, dancing, and drinking. Everybody who was anybody was there, and even I couldn't help but look around in a starstruck daze.

Steph laughed and grabbed my elbow, leading me towards the table with the place cards.

"You're sure I'm supposed to be here?" I

whispered, suddenly terrified.

"Yes, I'm sure. Look. Here's your card." She handed me a folded piece of robin's-egg-blue linen cardstock with my name printed across it. I was stunned. Until that moment, I'd been certain there was going to be some kind of monumentally embarrassing mix-up.

Card in hand, we walked to the dining area to put down our purses. There were fairy lights strung everywhere, making the whole scene look like it was right out of a Hollywood movie, which it pretty much was. I saw the leads from two of my favourite films and one of my favourite writers before we even reached our table. I took off my wrap and draped it over the back of my seat. Then I turned around.

Nothing could have prepared me for the sight of Mason in a tuxedo. My breath caught the moment our eyes met. His eyes were piercing, curly hair tamed with product, and his perfect body beautifully clad in exquisite fabric that draped his frame.

The look on his face told me he was having similar thoughts about me. The way the smile spread lazily across his face led me to think he was having some other thoughts as well. He crossed the five steps between us and wrapped his arm around my waist, pulling me in for a kiss on the cheek.

"Don't even try to stop me," he whispered.

"You realize photographers from every major magazine and gossip site are here tonight, right?" I asked.

"Don't care."

"You don't, but I do."

He dropped his arm and looked at me sheepishly.

"Okay. Fine. I'll behave. For now. But I make no guarantees when this thing is over."

He looked around, then back at me with a hopeful expression.

"Think it's almost over?"

I laughed and swatted him across the chest.

"Can you introduce me to Ford Jackson?" I asked.

"Ouch. Bullet to the heart." Mason clutched his chest in mock hurt.

"Come on. He's like, 100 years old. I've just always loved his writing. And he's right there."

Steph cleared her throat, tactfully reminding us of her presence.

"Mason. Take the woman to meet her idol."

He glanced over at her and smiled.

"You look amazing, Steph."

"I always look amazing. Now go. And behave. You piss off my Katie and you'll be in big trouble."

"Ouch. Again. Where's your loyalty, woman?" Mason asked, laughing.

With that, he took my elbow and led me towards my idol.

*

At exactly six o'clock, everyone was seated and the first chords of music indicating the start of the ceremony sounded. I found a place towards the back among the grips and gaffers I'd beat at the poker table. They'd tried several times to win their money back to no avail. I was glad to see we could part friends.

The whole scene was a fairytale come true. Fence posts were installed to create an aisle, with white ribbon and tulle woven between them. The path was strewn with wildflowers, creating a breathtaking array of bright colours against the green grass. There must have been over five hundred people in attendance, each of them better dressed than the next. It was truly a sight to behold.

Dean was standing at the altar with his best man—his brother, I was told—and after the parade of celebrity bridesmaids, a hush fell over the crowd as Jessica came out of her tent and into view. She looked perfect—ivory silk dress, fitted in the bodice and falling around her legs in waves. Her veil was to her knees, and her hair was swept up with just a few of her signature curls hanging loose to frame her face.

I swallowed and held my breath as she began her walk down the aisle. I glanced over at Rufus, sitting beside me, and he was just as transfixed. Everyone was. After a second, the photographer started shooting. There was only one during the ceremony itself, Jessica's agent having struck a deal with the media outlets that they could shoot the reception so long as no one pulled out a camera when they took their vows.

When she reached the front, the music stopped and the minister began. The smile spread across my face. I loved weddings. I might not have had so much luck in love in my own life, but I still couldn't help being a hopeless romantic when it came to other people. Watching Jessica and Dean exchange vows, I saw the love between them clear as day. I felt a stab of guilt over my skepticism of celebrity unions because in this case, it was so obvious how crazy these two were about each other.

I scanned the crowd for Mason and spotted him in the second row, sitting between two guys I didn't recognize from the back. At just that moment, he turned his head and caught my eye. Our gazes locked and I have no idea how long it was before everyone erupted into cheers and the spell was broken. I shook myself out of it and cheered for the newlyweds as they came back up the aisle.

When I turned back to look for Mason, he was gone.

CHAPTER TWENTY-FIVE

After dinner but before dessert, I made my way to the kitchen to check on the cake. I weaved carefully through the stations, not wanting to get the dress dirty. I spotted Chef Jacques near the walk-in and headed straight for him. He saw me and smiled.

"Well, aren't you a vision," he said.

I smiled in return and gave him a quick hug and a two-cheek kiss.

"Your cake is fine. Don't worry. We will take care of everything," he assured me.

"I know. But this is my first big show, you know? I'm a little nervous."

"It's a masterpiece, Katie. I promise you. It will be the talk of the night."

I blushed, said a quick goodbye, and turned to leave the kitchen. As soon as I exited, I bumped right into Mason.

"Stalking me?" I asked.

"Absolutely," he replied, grinning.

I rolled my eyes but didn't stop him when he bent his head to kiss me. In fact, I may have melted into him as he wrapped his arms around my waist. I wasn't worried about the kitchen staff and there was no one else around. I was getting on a plane the next day and taking advantage of every chance I got. I almost whined when he drew away.

"You going to dance with me tonight?" he asked.

"Not excessively."

"But you will?"

"I will."

"Should we get back? They'll probably be serving cake soon," he said.

"I just came from the kitchen. We've got a few minutes."

I saw the gleam in his eye.

"What'd you have in mind?" he asked.

I took his hand and led him towards the back staircase, the one used for taking the trash out to the containers. I knew it wouldn't be used until the end of the day. I pushed open the door and stuck my head in, just to be sure.

Seeing no one, I walked in, pulling Mason behind me.

We were standing in a dim stairwell, lit only by the small window set into the door leading out back. I looked up at him and raised an eyebrow. That was all it took for him to push me back up against the wall and kiss me again with considerably more force this time.

"I don't remember this being on your list," he whispered in my ear.

"Last-minute addition."

I tilted my face back up towards his as I felt his hand slide up my leg underneath my dress. I moaned and draped one arm over his shoulder, as much to pull him closer as to hold me up.

"Have I told you how hot this dress looks on you?"

"No, you haven't."

"Fuck, Katie. I wanted to tear it off the second I saw you."

He kissed a line down my neck and I was suddenly grateful for the plunging neckline. While one hand worked my panties down, his other hand slid into the dress to cup my right breast. I pushed myself back into the wall as he freed it and dipped his head to take my nipple in his mouth.

"Oh, fuck, Mason."

I tried to kick off my shoes and he grabbed my leg.

"Leave them on," he growled.

He reluctantly let go of my breast to ease the dress up around my waist. I held it for him as he slid my panties down, tucking them into his pocket with a wink before unbuckling his pants. I reached forward to help him and as I worked the zipper, he took my face in his hands and kissed me again.

"I'm going to miss you," he whispered.

"Shhh."

"This has been so much fun."

Fun. My heart sank. That's all it was. Fun. No matter what I'd told myself, what I was feeling was far beyond *fun*. Despite my precautions and our little arrangement, I'd let myself fall for the guy. I bit my lower lip, hard, to bring myself back into the moment. His hands on my body. His mouth on my neck.

I widened my stance and his hand slid between my legs, erasing all thought and reason from my mind. I lay my head back against the wall and moaned softly, prompting him to cover my mouth with his own. I parted my lips, anxious to have him as close as humanly possible.

"I want you," I whispered.

He pushed my hair behind my ears and took

my face in both hands, looking me straight in the eye.

"You've got me."

Meaningless words uttered during sex. Another shot through the heart. I closed my eyes and tilted my face up and he responded with another hungry kiss. I wrapped my arms around his waist, drawing him closer. He reached down to free himself, and I followed his lead, wrapping my hand around his hard length and stroking him until his breath grew heavy in my ear. I smiled to myself as he mumbled his first *Oh, God.* I took the condom he'd pulled from his pocket, tore the foil, and slipped it on. Then I brought him home, grinding my hips up against his.

He grabbed my wrists, pinning them up against the wall by my head. He groaned somewhere deep in his chest as he as began to move with me. He paused momentarily as we heard two voices leaving the kitchen, heading in our direction.

"Mason—"

"Shh."

He began to move again, building up his rhythm as the two men passed directly outside the door.

"Oh. . ."

He dropped one wrist to cover my mouth

with his hand. He increased his speed until he was thrusting into me. I brought one leg up and wrapped it around his waist as I bit down on his hand to stop from crying out. The men had stopped a few feet away, arguing over whether they'd left the stove on or not. The room grew dizzy as their voices faded. All I could see or feel was Mason, bringing me closer and closer to the edge.

He pulled his hand away from my mouth and replaced it with his lips, his tongue dancing against mine as I felt his body tense. I reached down with my free hand to touch myself, not wanting to make him wait any longer. He groaned as he realized what I was doing and slowed his speed. He pulled his head away, and we looked deep into each other's eyes.

"Katie."

It was all I needed. My entire body erupted as the orgasm tore through me. He followed quickly, his hands dropping to my waist as we both rode out the waves together. He dipped his head and his mouth found mine once again, kissing me gently as we both came down.

I let my leg fall and eventually he pulled away. He grinned sheepishly as he did up his pants. I put my hand out for my panties and he shook his head firmly.

"Nope. No way. They stay in my pocket."

"Are you crazy?"

"Maybe. But it's my last night. I wanna make sure I've got easy access."

"I'm only letting you get away with this because you're a great lay. Tell me. Are all movie stars this good?"

I burst out laughing as his mouth dropped open. He reached out and swatted me playfully. I reached up to block him and he grabbed my wrist, pulling me in for another kiss. When we came up for air, I realized the voices had gone.

"I guess they left," I said.

Mason shrugged.

We got ourselves decent again and he poked his head out the doorway to ensure the coast was clear before we made our escape. He opened the side exit door and grabbed my hand, pulling me outside. And that's when the cameras started going.

CHAPTER TWENTY-SIX

"Mason! Who's your girlfriend?"

"Mason! Can we get a picture?"

"Mason! Mason!"

They swarmed around us, cameras going off at a million miles an hour. Mason instinctively reached for me, grabbing me around the waist to pull me closer, but I pulled away. The last thing I wanted was to give them fodder.

"Hey, guys, give us some space, okay?" Mason pushed his way through the crowd and in the distance I saw Noah, his driver, jogging up to rescue us.

"Hey! Come on! Give them some room. There's no story here! Katie is with the caterers," Noah cried.

Shit.

While the two of them were dealing with the press, I slipped away and headed for safety back in the kitchen.

"Katie! Katie! Can we get a last name?"

I ducked into the doors and raced down the hall to the kitchen, where I found Chef Jacques standing by a trolley with the cake. His expression told me exactly how panicked I must've looked. He ran to my side.

"Katie. What's wrong?"

I shook my head, unable to speak. I glanced at the cake and the clock on the wall.

"Go. Take it. I'm fine."

"Are you sure? Don't you want to be there?"

Again, I shook my head, wanting nothing but to be back in the safety of my hotel room, packing for my trip home.

"No. Go. Tell me how it went later."

He threw me one last concerned look and then wheeled the cake out with the help of his pastry chef and sous-chef. I watched it disappear through the double doors and waited a few minutes before following them. I needed a moment to collect myself, plus another moment to make sure the press was gone.

*

As soon as I got back to my room, I pulled my suitcase out of the closet and started throwing my clothes in. I knew I had to stop and take a breath, but the need to get out was overwhelming. As the minutes rolled by, however, I started questioning whether anything truly horrific had happened. Yes, they had pictures of me with Mason. Yes, they knew my first name. Yes, they knew I was the caterer. But the whole thing had transpired in less than two minutes. Surely it was forgotten about?

Right. I'm caught red-handed with a notoriously single A-list actor and everyone is just going to forget about it. I took a deep breath and kept packing. The knock on the door came a few minutes later.

"You have a key," I said.

"Can I use it?" Mason asked through the door.

"Why not?"

I watched the handle turn as he pushed the door open and walked hesitantly towards me. His expression was pitiful and my heart melted at the sight. I bit my lip and rolled my eyes.

"I'm not mad at you," I assured him.

"But you're mad."

"Am I mad? You spent countless hours

telling me this is exactly why you don't date, and now here we are. Am I going to be on the cover of every tabloid tomorrow? Did I bring misery upon my small town? Did I destroy my business, into which I just brought my two best friends as partners? Yes. It's safe to say I'm mad."

"I'm sorry, Katie. I really am." He stood there, helplessly watching me pack. "Your flight's not leaving any earlier, you know."

"I was thinking maybe I'd try to get an earlier one."

He reached out and gently took my wrist, stopping me from zipping up my case.

"You're leaving in the morning. That's soon enough. Come back to the wedding with me."

"Are you kidding?"

Mason sighed, realizing he wasn't going to win this one. He kicked off his shoes, loosened his tie, and climbed up onto my bed.

"What are you doing?" I asked.

"Getting comfortable."

"You have a wedding reception to get to."

"I'm good."

I stared at him, exasperated.

"What do you mean, you're good? Your co-star is out there celebrating one of the biggest milestones in her life."

"And after tonight, I don't know if I'll ever

see you again. I'm staying here."

"You're serious?"

"Dead."

I laughed in disbelief. Mason Scott would rather be hanging out in my hotel room than at the biggest celebrity event of the year. The fact that it was the last time we'd be together was something I'd just have to set aside for the moment. I cocked my head, looked at him, and said, "You want the dress on or off?"

CHAPTER TWENTY-SEVEN

The flight home was a welcome respite. Mason and I hadn't slept a wink the entire night, and as soon as I settled into my seat, I closed my eyes and tried to doze off. Within seconds, there was a tap on my shoulder. I looked up and there was a flight attendant standing over me.

"Katie Simon?" she asked.

"Yeah..."

She flashed a bright smile and indicated I should stand.

"Is there a problem?" I asked.

"Not at all," she assured me. "Just follow me, please."

I got up and collected my stuff, smiling

apologetically at my seatmate as I climbed over him. I followed the flight attendant down the aisle and she pulled back the curtain heading into business class. I looked at her, unsure. Once again, she smiled and handed me a note. I took it. It read: *It's the least I could do. M.*

I smiled to myself and strode through the curtain. There was another attendant waiting at my seat and I slid into it, made myself comfortable, and gratefully accepted the glass of champagne. Once I'd dispensed with that, I closed my eyes and fell asleep.

*

I made the mistake of checking the Internet gossip sites while waiting at the airport for the car production had arranged to take me home. Every homepage had a picture of Mason and me, hand in hand, laughing and looking straight into the camera. The headlines were variations of *Who is Katie Simon?* and *Is Katie Simon Mason Scott's Secret Girlfriend?*

I shoved my phone in my pocket and looked up to see if I could spot the car. Instead, I saw several reporters rushing towards me, cameras at the ready.

"Katie! Do you have a minute?"

Just then, the car pulled up and the driver

hopped out. He ran around the car, grabbed my bag, and opened the door. I slid in and he shut the door behind me, stopping to drop my bag in the trunk before resuming his place in the driver's seat.

"Sorry I was late, Miss. Wrong terminal." He looked at the crowd gathering outside the car. "Looks like I got here just in time, though."

A few minutes earlier would've been better.

"Yeah, thanks," I muttered.

The drive from the airport up to Mountain Valley was about an hour and a half. I spent the bulk of it staring out the window, wondering how much the press knew. Clearly someone had tipped them off about my flight and where I lived. I wondered briefly whether it had been Rufus or Craig one of the other guys I'd beat at poker, but dismissed the idea. They were decent guys.

"There's a back entrance to my building. I can access it through a small path around the corner. Can you drop me off there?" I asked the driver.

"What about your bag?" he asked.

"I can manage. I just don't want to risk there being anyone out front. And if you drive past, they'll notice the car for sure. Can't remember the last time anyone around here saw a Lincoln

Town Car."

The driver laughed quietly and nodded his head. He glanced at me in the rearview.

"Everything okay?"

"Yeah. I'll live."

He did as asked, and after he handed me my bag, I made my way through the brush until I was in the small alley behind my building. I unlocked the back door and made my way in. When I got up to my apartment, I dropped my bag, stripped off my clothes, and walked straight into the shower. Then I crashed.

*

I was up before the alarm at 3:45 a.m., which was essentially 10:00 a.m. Swiss time. I felt okay, except for the fact that I'd lost a day somewhere. I rolled out of bed and peered out the window. The street was dark and deserted and I could see my mountains rising up around the bend in the road. I smiled to myself as I picked up my phone.

I stared at the black screen for a moment, then put it back down. There was no need to upset myself before I'd even had any coffee. I'd get up, shower, grab a quick breakfast and then head to the bakery. I'd be late, but since they weren't expecting me in at all today, I figured I

211

was in the clear. Well, that plus I was now an object of global curiosity.

I made my way through the pre-dawn streets of my beloved small town, all the while wondering what kind of hell I was about to bring down on it. By the time I got to the bakery, I could see Tess and Jax hard at work through the glass windows. I took a deep breath and walked in through the front door.

"KATIE!" Tess screamed, running over and sweeping me up in a huge hug.

Jax looked up and ran out from the kitchen, throwing his arms around the two of us until we were just one mass of bodies and laughter and tears.

"Girl! You really know how to make a splash!" Jax laughed.

I extricated myself from the love fest and looked at them both with worry in my eyes.

"How bad is it?"

They exchanged a quick glance.

"It's bad," Tess admitted. "But we'll be fine. It's great publicity for the bakery. We were packed all day yesterday. But look at you! You look amazing! Your hair!"

I shrugged off her compliments, more important matters on my mind.

"I can't even bear to open my phone this morning."

"Screw that," Jax said. "We need details. On the hair, yes, but more importantly, on the movie star!"

I hesitated only a moment before answering, "I slept with him."

The collective gasp made me laugh, despite my misery.

"I knew it," Tess said. "I can't believe you didn't tell us. How was it?"

"Tess, that's irrelevant at the moment, don't you think? Look at this mess I'm in."

"It is NOT irrelevant, but whatever," Jax interrupted. "Don't worry about this mess. Like Tess said, so far it's been great for business. And we've already got a plan."

I looked at him suspiciously.

"A plan?"

Tess nodded her head enthusiastically.

"Yes! A brilliant plan. These idiots are only interested in you because they think you're dating Mason Scott. All you need is a boyfriend—or a decoy boyfriend," she said off my look. "Just think about it. It's brilliant. They see you with someone else, they forget all about you."

I thought about it for a moment. She wasn't wrong. The only interest the press had in me was directly tied to Mason. If I could show there was no tie, there'd be no interest. I walked through to the back, washed up, and tied on my apron. I was still mulling over the idea when I pulled the last tray of cinnamon buns out of the oven two hours later.

The early customers came in for their coffee and everyone was excited to see me. Of course, they'd all heard the news that I was going off to bake a celebrity wedding cake, but the Internet gossip was more excitement than many of them had had in their entire life. They bombarded me with questions and I kept my good humour, remembering these were the people my livelihood depended upon.

The first reporter walked in at nine, but by then I was prepared. There were about a dozen people in the shop waiting to be served, but she walked right up to me while her photographer started walking around the shop taking pictures.

"Katie? Have you got time for a few questions?" the reporter asked.

"Sure," I said. "Are you interested in the cinnamon buns or the freshly-baked muffins?"

Everyone laughed. She looked around, unsure, then gathered her confidence.

"You know why I'm here. Why don't you tell me about Mason?"

"I'm sorry," I said. "I've really got nothing to say. I was hired to bake Jessica Thompson's wedding cake. That's it, really." I turned to serve another customer.

"Oh, come on, we all saw the pictures. How did you end up with Mason?"

"Listen. I've got a lot of customers here right now. If you'd like to buy something, I'd be happy to serve you. Just grab a number."

The reporter bit her lip in frustration then went to talk to her photographer. They conferred in the corner while I put a half-dozen croissants into a paper bag for Mrs. Harris. She shot one last look at me over her shoulder before they both walked out. I breathed out a sigh of relief. Mrs. Harris handed me a twenty and smiled.

"You did good, Katie. Don't let the bastards get you down," she said.

I smiled at her saucy language, something the 83-year-old matriarch was known for.

"Was he a nice boy?" she asked. "That's all that really matters."

I reached out and touched her shoulder.

"He was nice. But there's nothing there. Really. I doubt I'll ever even speak to him again."

"Hm," she grunted. "That's a shame."

She turned to leave and as I moved to serve the next customer, Jax stuck his head out from the kitchen and called to me, "There's a phone call for you. A Jack Roth."

"Don't know him," I said. "Probably another reporter. Take a message."

Tess and I got through the morning rush and I retreated back into the kitchen to make some sandwiches for the lunch crowd. Once again, I was thankful for the small town and resulting lack of dining options. A few more reporters came in, but mostly there were photographers camped in the square across the street.

"Think they're waiting for Mason to show up?" Jax asked.

"Ha. They'll be waiting a long time."

"Oh, yeah?"

"Yeah. Jax. There's nothing between us. It was a fling. *Fun*, as he was fond of saying."

"Katie, I've known you a long time. Fun was never in your vocabulary when it came to men. You are not a fling girl."

"Maybe not, but for once in my life I saw something I wanted and I took it. I don't regret it. Do I miss him? Of course, I do. But it was a fantasy. This is my reality. Now, how are we going to find me a fake boyfriend?"

Jax stared at me for a moment and then pulled a folded sheet of paper from his back pocket.

"I've made a list. I figure you could go on a date with each of them, see if something

216

clicks."

"I thought the idea was a fake boyfriend."

Jax hesitated, and at that moment Tess walked into the kitchen.

"That is the idea," she said. "But if you happen to meet someone you actually like, well, all the better, no?"

"I don't know. Sounds like you two are taking advantage of a shitty situation to try and set me up."

They exchanged a glance.

"Yup. Just like I thought. Sadly, I'm not in the position to argue." I looked out through the glass windows to the square across the street, still littered with photographers. "Okay? Who's first? I'm free for dinner."

CHAPTER TWENTY-EIGHT

By the time three o'clock rolled around, the jet lag had hit me like a ton of bricks. I was useless at the shop, so I opted to go home and grab a quick nap before dinner. Jax had wasted no time setting me up with the first guy on his list, someone named Jake Fitch.

I got home and crashed on the couch. I never even made it to the bedroom. When I opened my eyes, the early evening sun coming through the window told me I had very little time to get ready. I jumped up and glanced at the clock as I headed for the shower. Almost six. I was meeting Jake at seven.

I had finished my hair and makeup and was searching for a small, cute bag to wear when it struck me I still hadn't turned on my phone. I looked around for it, spotting it on the hallway table. I took a deep breath and hit the power button. But before I could even open a browser window, my home screen was bombarded with a wall of texts. All from Mason. Mainly wanting to know if I was okay and why I hadn't gotten in touch with him.

I had to do this right before my date?

I sat down and thought for a moment before typing.

Hey. Sorry. My phone was off for a few days. Everything's fine, really. But maybe it would be easier if you didn't text me?

I didn't want to be harsh, but I also knew the easiest way to do this was to just go cold turkey. I was nobody, but we'd all read the stories about the British tabloids hacking into cell phones. I wanted to keep myself clean, no roads leading back to Mason.

I dropped the phone into my pocket and walked out the front door. I was still tired, but determined to go meet Jake, and hopefully make the best of it.

*

"Katie Simon? Is that you?"

I was standing in front of *Les Trois Canards*, a

cosy little French restaurant on the road out of town. I turned to see a man, a few inches taller than me, with blond hair cropped close and smiling blue eyes.

"Do I know you?" I asked, confused.

"I'm Jake. Nah, I guess you wouldn't know me. We never actually met," he conceded.

"But you know me?"

"Damn straight. We went to school together. I was halfback on the football team, but two years ahead of you. But the highlight of my high school career was when I paid two bucks to see your bra in the guys' locker room."

"WHAT?"

I was mortified. I had *never* heard this story before. Jake took one look at my face and realized his faux pas.

"Shit," he said. "I'm sorry. I thought you knew about that. Can we start again?"

He walked up to me and held out his hand.

"Hi. I'm Jake. You must be Katie. So nice to finally meet. Jax has told me a lot about you."

I eyed him skeptically but eventually put on my hand to shake his. He flashed me a brilliant smile.

"Come," he said. "Let's eat."

He turned and opened the restaurant door, indicating I should lead the way.

Despite its inauspicious beginnings, the date didn't turn out half bad. Turns out Jake left Mountain Valley for college immediately after graduation and then took a job coaching football at a resort-town high school about 20 minutes away. He was a nice enough guy, asked me plenty of questions about the bakery and the film shoot, and I finally got the story of how he came to pay two bucks to see my bra.

Apparently, my lab partner in science had been pissed at me for a low grade we'd gotten on an assignment and swiped my bra while I was in gym one day. I didn't even remember the incident, probably because I always had a spare in my locker. To Jake's memory, at least thirty-five guys had lined up that day to see it, a number that shocked me given I'd only had one boyfriend during the entire five years. I assumed it just meant they were more interested in my underwear than in me.

But the conversation always led back to football. It was clearly his favourite topic. When we weren't talking about it directly, he was making some kind of sports analogy that loosely pertained to the issue at hand. Given that I didn't know the first thing about the game, he found himself laughing alone at his own jokes quite a bit. Didn't seem to bother him.

I worked my way through three or four drinks over the course of the meal, so I was more than happy to have him walk me home before he hit the highway.

"Didn't you ever think of leaving?" he asked as we passed by the bakery's darkened windows.

"Of course, I did. And I still do sometimes. But that little bakery means everything to me. I could never have just abandoned it. My grandma trusted me with it."

"You were saying over dinner that you just brought on partners? I don't think you ever finished that story."

No, I hadn't. Because he'd brought up some team trade and completely derailed the conversation.

"Yes. That's right. Kind of you to remember. My two best friends. They've been working for me forever. We're going to be signing the partnership papers this week."

"Well that should free you up to travel some, no? Maybe now you'll be able to get away and explore the world."

I looked at him and laughed.

"The world, huh? You ended up two towns over."

He clutched his heart like I'd shot him.

"Ouch! Though I suppose you're right. But it's still not the same as standing still."

I thought about that. He had a point. He'd left and hadn't returned. Well, except for the odd date, I guessed. And Mason had made the same point about my time being freed up. *Mason.* I'd gone the entire evening without thinking about him. As we approached my building, I saw a couple of stray photographers hanging out.

"Listen," I said. "I had a really nice time tonight. Thanks so much."

He smiled and took my hand in both of his, turning to give me his full attention.

"So did I."

I glanced over his shoulder, taking note of the photographers, shooting away behind him.

"You realize there are photographers over there, right?" I leaned in to whisper in his ear.

"I know," he nodded. "I saw the bits in the paper. Didn't think it necessary to bring it up."

I pulled back and grinned.

"That was very decent of you, Jake."

He shrugged.

"I assume you've heard enough about it already. And if the rumours were true, you wouldn't be out on a date with me." He paused. "Want me to kiss you goodnight? Just

223

to get them off the scent?"

It was like he'd read my mind.

"Actually, that would be great. But I just, I don't want you to think—"

"Means nothing, I get it. I like you. I just wanna help out."

I laughed out loud, throwing back my head and letting loose for the first time in days. He then grabbed me around the waist and pulled me in, all dramatic-like, and kissed me. It was a very nice kiss, and I wish I could say I saw fireworks, but I didn't. In fact, when I closed my eyes, all I saw was Mason.

CHAPTER TWENTY-NINE

When I got into work the next morning, Jax was anxiously awaiting an update. Clearly, he'd already seen the pictures on the Internet and was practically jumping up and down with glee when I walked through the door.

"I knew you'd hit it off!" he screamed.

I rolled my eyes and walked through to the kitchen. He trailed me like an eager puppy. I said nothing as I washed my hands and then pulled on an apron. He was hopping from foot to foot, just watching me. Finally, I turned to him.

"What?"

"WHAT? What happened?"

"Nothing happened. We went to dinner. He

talked about football. He walked me home. We saw the photographers and he was a gentleman and offered to kiss me."

As soon as the words were out of my mouth, I knew how ridiculous they sounded. But it was the truth. Jax stared at me, jaw agape.

"A gentleman? I saw that kiss, Katie."

"Yes, hopefully everyone saw it. What did the headline say?"

Jax pulled out his phone and pulled up a gossip site before handing it over to me. I took it from him and glanced at the screen. *Mason Scott not good enough for Katie Simon? Small town girl finds new love.*

"Huh," I said. "That's actually pretty perfect. Great."

I handed him back his phone and got to work.

"So?" he said. "Are you seeing him again?"

"Who? Jake? No. I told you, there was nothing there."

"Okay, then. I'll line up the next one."

I turned to look at him, elbow deep in a shaggy dough.

"No. Don't. It's fine. The plan worked."

"Well, your plan maybe. Not mine."

"I'm not interested. Leave it alone."

We worked together in a tense silence until Tess came in at opening. The morning crowd came and went without a photographer or reporter in sight. I couldn't believe how easy it had been. Sometime before noon, Jax poked his head out of the kitchen to tell me Jack Roth had called again. Well, one reporter was being persistent. Didn't mean I had to respond, though.

Right before the lunch rush started, a guy walked in. He was around my height, but incredibly well-built. His arms were huge, and I could see the muscle ripple underneath his T-shirt as he gently closed the front door behind him. He had brown curly hair, light grey eyes, and a funny little smile that he graced me with for a millisecond before walking over hesitantly.

"Katie?"

"Yes—?"

"Hi, I'm Chance. Did Jax tell you I was coming?"

I took a deep breath and glanced over my shoulder, throwing an annoyed look at Jax before turning back to Chance.

"No. He did not, and while I appreciate—"

Just then Jax ran out from the kitchen and threw an arm around my shoulder.

"Katie! Katie, in all the excitement over the past couple days, Tess and I forgot to tell you we hired an employee. Katie, this is Chance.

Chance, Katie."

I looked from Jax to Chance, then over at Tess, who was grinning stupidly from ear to ear. Of course they both wanted to hire this guy. He was gorgeous. And gorgeous in a weirdly attainable way. Leave it to these two.

"Hi, Chance. It's really nice to meet you. I assume you've got some experience working in a bakery?"

"Yes. Of course. I recently moved her from Montreal, where I ran a commercial bakery that served over forty establishments in the greater Montreal region. I am a proud graduate of St. Pius X's culinary school, where I also took extra courses in pastry."

I stared at him, speechless. The guy had more experience than I did.

"Oh. Well, then. It's great to have you on board. Is this your first day?"

Tess finally felt it appropriate to jump in.

"No, he's been with us over a week now. It's been great. I totally meant to tell you, but I didn't expect two weeks to pass by without hearing from you." Tess shot me a look that made me bite my tongue on my next comment. I retreated into the kitchen to have a word with Jax.

"So, what's the deal? He's in back with you, I assume?"

Jax blushed.

"Well, yeah. He doesn't have much counter experience."

"And not that it's any of my business, but are you—?"

"No, dammit. He's straight."

I laughed.

"Sorry. Tess got an eye on him?"

Jax shrugged.

"I don't think so. He's nice to look at, but they don't seem to have much in common." He paused before continuing. "You're not mad we hired someone without you, are you? We just really needed the help, and it's only a matter of time until the papers are signed—"

"Jax, it's fine. You seem to have made a great choice. I am not at all mad. Relieved, actually, that I don't have to take care of it. This is the first time it's really sunk in that this place isn't solely my responsibility anymore. It's quite a liberating feeling, actually."

I let out a little laugh as I thought about it. I returned to the front to help Tess with the customers as the lunch crowd poured in. The press was gone. I was back home. I had two great partners and a new employee. Things were looking up.

CHAPTER THIRTY

The week flew by. The partnership papers got signed and the three of us went out for a fancy dinner with lots of champagne to seal the deal. So much, in fact, that the owner came out to see what the grand celebration was all about. It was a fairly new restaurant and it was our first time there. None of us had met the owner, which was rare in a small town, but nevertheless he sat down with us and accepted our offer of a glass.

His name was Adam, and he looked to be in his mid-thirties. He had dirty blond hair that fell around his ears and the saddest brown eyes I'd ever seen. He didn't seem sad, though maybe slightly reserved. He'd taken a seat next to Tess and hadn't taken his eyes off of her since sitting down. She seemed equally smitten and I sipped my champagne, shooting covert looks at Jax.

Over the next few weeks, the four of us fell into a new groove. We worked surprisingly well together. It had been the three of us for so long I was worried what a fourth would do, but my worries were completely unfounded. Chance was a dream come true and the more he did in the kitchen, the later I got to sleep in.

One morning in late August, I was walking to work at a leisurely pace when I passed by the old Merson warehouse. This was a building I'd passed almost every day for as long as I could remember, and it had always stood empty. I remembered my grandmother telling me stories about the war, and how the warehouse was used to house artillery and supplies for soldiers before it got shipped out. But for as long as I'd been alive, it had sat vacant.

As kids, we all used to go in on dares. It was like a rite of passage. As adolescents, it became the number one make-out spot in town. When you live in an area surrounded by nature and mountains, a run-down warehouse with decrepit floors and sagging ceilings becomes very attractive as a secret hideaway. Which I guess is why in our teenage years it became the place to experiment with cigarettes, drugs, and alcohol. But it was vacant when I was born, and I always assumed it would remain that way long after I was gone.

But that August morning, as I walked past, there was a construction permit hanging in one of the windows, and a "SOLD" banner strewn across the rusted For Sale sign. I stood in shock, my first thought being sympathy for the generations of kids who'd grow up in Mountain Valley without Merson's warehouse. My next thought was disbelief that someone had actually bought the place.

I walked into work with one of the morning regulars, Lacey Palmer. She flashed me a quick smile and held the door open for me. Divorced with two kids, Lacey's favourite thing to do was drop them off at school and then come for a coffee and pastry. I'd noticed ever since Chance started, she'd been adding a little makeup to her morning routine. *Good for her.*

As I washed up and tied on my apron, I looked over at Tess and asked if she'd notice the Merson place.

"I did. Weird, huh? I didn't think that place would ever sell."

"Any idea who bought it?" I asked.

"Nope. It's a mystery. Everyone's talking

about it, though. I'm impressed, actually. Pretty hard to keep a secret in a town this size."

"Well, it's obviously an outsider."

Tess nodded in agreement, then silently thrust her chin in Lacey's direction. She was standing by the kitchen, chatting with Chance about which pie she should bring home that day.

"Come on," I whispered. "It's cute. And Lord knows that woman deserves some happiness."

"And what about you? And your happiness?" Tess asked.

"What do you mean? I'm happy."

"Come on, Katie. I've known you too long. You haven't said one word about Mason since you've been back. And I know you like to play your cards close to your chest, but this is beyond. Even for you. It's like you've erased his existence."

I waited for Lacey to choose her pie, pay for it, and leave before turning back to Tess.

"I have erased his existence. What other choice do I have? He's gone. He's so gone that sometimes I wonder if it ever really happened."

"You mean he hasn't called?" she asked, clearly confused.

"He did. He texted me a bunch of times. But

I asked him to stop. I was worried about the press. I just wanted to move on. I thought it would be easier."

"And—?"

I shrugged. The phone rang. I glanced through to the kitchen and saw both guys elbow-deep in batter. The shop was empty so I picked it up.

"Hi, this is Franni's."

"Hi, is this Katie?"

"Yes, it is. How can I help you?"

"Thank goodness. I have been trying to reach you for weeks. This is Jack Roth."

Shit.

"Listen, Mr. Roth, I'm not sure what this is about—"

"This is about Grace Atkinson's wedding in three months. She wants one of your cakes. Can you do it?"

I stopped short. *Grace Atkinson?* Even I knew that name. She was the female equivalent of Mason in Hollywood, one of the hottest commodities around. I caught a glimpse of her at Jessica's wedding, but hadn't realized she was even engaged.

"I'm sorry. Who is this again?"

"Jack. Jack Roth. I'm Grace's manager. Like I said, it's been hell getting hold of you. I'd have moved on, but Grace insisted after

Jessica's wedding that she have the same pastry chef. Glad I finally caught you."

Tess looked at the expression on my face and gently took the phone from my hand. She spoke quietly into the receiver, listened, then grabbed a pen to take down the details. When she hung up the phone, she stared at me a full thirty seconds before screaming at the top of her lungs, "YOU MADE IT, BABY!"

CHAPTER THIRTY-ONE

After making a deal with Jack, the calls started to roll in. A trend was a trend, and Jessica Thompson was certainly a trendsetter. Jax, Chance, and Tess were beside themselves with excitement. I was a little numb from shock. Luckily, the events were spaced out and all on this side of the Atlantic Ocean, the majority of them being in California.

"You know," Tess said. "I was looking at the calendar, and it wouldn't be a stupid idea to rent an AirBnB or something in LA for a few weeks in October. Seems to be a busy month for you there."

"I was kind of thinking the same thing. I've never been to California, and with what these guys are paying—"

"Plus, you can really use the vacation," Jax added, emptying a tray of cheese danish into the case.

"Where did you come from?" I asked, laughing.

"The kitchen. You know, that place you never go anymore."

I stopped laughing immediately. Jax was right. Ever since Chance had come into our lives, I'd pretty much stopped baking.

"Hey," I said. "Let's switch shifts tomorrow, okay? I'll come in at four and work with Chance."

"Itching to get your hands dirty again?" Jax asked, twinkle in his eye.

"I am now."

He smiled and tousled my hair as he walked past me back toward the kitchen.

"You got it, partner. I'll never say no to a sleep-in."

*

The next morning I was up before the alarm, actually excited to get back into the kitchen. I'd spent so much time planning wedding cakes and organizing my schedule that it felt like forever since I'd had the quiet of the morning to knead dough, shape rolls, and press out pie crusts.

Chance was remarkably easy to get along with. We chatted all morning as we worked in perfect unison, like a well-choreographed ballet. I was glad for the distraction. As well as things were going professionally, I still found myself thinking about Mason. No matter how many times I told myself I had gotten exactly what I asked for, it didn't help. I was the one who set the rules, I was the one who had made the decision. But I couldn't stop wondering why he hadn't tried a little harder.

I had never been one to play games. It just wasn't my style. So when I told him not to contact me, I had meant it. I just never thought it would be so easy for him. Everything we had done together had seemed so real at the time that I couldn't understand how he was able to walk away without a fight. Maybe he was just that good an actor.

We finished early and Chance suggested we bake a few extra dozen croissants, as he'd noticed they'd been selling out early the past few days. He pulled the dough from the walk-in and we got to work at the table, flouring the surface and pulling out our rolling pins. I stood silently watching him form his croissant and shook my head.

"You know, in all the years I've been making croissant, I always thought I did a fine job. Then I see yours and mine look like they were rolled by a three-year-old."

Chance laughed and cleared a space on the countertop.

"Come here, I'll show you."

I walked around to his side of the table and he moved behind me, taking each of my hands in his as if he were giving me a golf lesson.

"It's really simple, actually. Just make sure you start tightly at the base and keep a uniform pressure. You want it tight, but you also want enough air to get in for that light, flaky texture. No one wants a dense croissant."

I looked over my shoulder at him and laughed. He gave me a quick headbutt and I turned back to the work at hand. We both jumped when we heard the tap on the front door.

"Shit," Chance said. "It's not even five yet."

We both looked up and my heart stopped. There on the sidewalk stood Mason, dressed in a T-shirt and faded blue jeans with a baseball hat drawn low over his head.

"Holy shit. Is that—" Chance asked.

"Yup," I said, interrupting him.

I stood there for a moment while I tried to remember how to breathe. Chance stepped away from me and slowly untied his apron, hanging it back up on its hook.

"What are you doing?" I asked, still not having made a move toward the door. I could see Mason looking at me, a silent, pleading expression on his face.

"I've got an errand to run. I'll be back later."

With that, Chance slipped through out the back door, leaving me all alone. I licked my lips, drew myself up, and made my way to the front. I unlocked the door and looked up at him, silent.

"Am I interrupting you?"

I shook my head.

"It kind of looked like I was interrupting you."

"What do you want, Mason?"

He grinned sheepishly.

"I had a hankering for some cinnamon buns. I thought maybe we could make some."

*

I let Mason in and locked the door behind him. I was still trying to recover and couldn't think of anything intelligent to say.

"We're done baking for the morning," I said.

"Jesus Christ, Katie. I'm here to see you."

"Why?"

"Why? Because I miss you, dammit. I can't stop thinking about you. Every night I dream about our time together and every day I wake up and wonder what you're doing. And I know this is selfish of me. You asked me to not even text you, and then I show up at your door. But when I saw those pictures of you and that guy, I just couldn't give up without even —"

I cut him off with a kiss. I threw my arms around him and planted my mouth on his, running my tongue along his bottom lip until he gathered me up in his arms and kissed me back. We melted into each other, and I have no idea how much time passed before we came up for air.

"You missed me, too?" he asked hopefully.

I laughed.

"Yes, I missed you, too."

"Oh, thank God."

At just that moment, the front door burst open and Jax came striding in.

"You know, I tried, but I just couldn't sleep in. Figured once I was up, I may as well come in and. . .Holy shit."

Jax stopped dead in his tracks when he saw me in Mason's arms and a huge smile lit up his face. I gave him a sheepish look in return.

"Mason and I are going to take a walk. You

got this? Chance will be back in a few."

Jax just nodded, still grinning like an idiot as Mason and I walked out the front door.

CHAPTER THIRTY-TWO

Once we were outside, things got a little awkward again between us. We walked silently for a bit and he reached for my hand, then changed his mind. I smiled to myself at his uncertainty, marvelling that a movie star was trying to figure out how to play it cool with the girl from the northern Canadian town. I took his hand and put him out of his misery.

"That guy just now, he wasn't the same guy as the one in the picture," Mason said.

"No, that's Chance. He works for us. And he was showing me how to roll the perfect croissant."

He nodded curtly.

"And the guy from the picture—?"

"Was a decoy to throw the press of my trail."

Mason stopped short, then burst out laughing.

"Well, that worked beautifully, didn't it?"

I laughed along with him, happy he saw it for what it was.

"See?" he said, turning to me, "you're a natural at this."

We'd arrived at the main intersection in town and I made an impulsive decision to turn right. He followed without question, jogging a few paces to catch up with me.

"Where we going?" he asked.

"You'll see."

We passed a few early morning cyclists, joggers, and fitness enthusiasts getting an early start on their day.

"So what's going on with you?" I asked.

"Well, I just signed for the lead in a great thriller. I start shooting in October."

"Where?"

"LA. I'm thankful, actually. I've got a bunch of side projects coming up and I'd rather not be on location for a while."

My heart sank at the idea that he wouldn't be around Mountain Valley if he didn't want to travel, but on the other hand, I was going to be in LA in October. I decided to keep that information in my back pocket for the time being.

"Who else is in it?" I asked.

"They haven't finished casting, but I know they want Hannah Lee and Mark Jackson for the other two leads."

"Wow. That would be quite the casting coup."

"Yeah. Hey. Where are we going?"

We stopped outside the Merson warehouse and I cocked my head, giving him a mischievous smile.

"This is the old Merson warehouse," I said. "It's been empty for as long as I've been alive. It's also been a rite of passage for everyone who grew up in this town."

"Really?" he said. "Looks like a run-down collection of shacks to me."

"More to it than meets the eye," I said, taking his hand.

We walked through the overgrowth along what was once a path leading up to the main entrance of the building. I turned away from the front doors and made straight for the open window off to the side, hidden behind the tree.

"Impressive," Mason whistled.

"I told you. Rite of passage."

We carefully stepped through the window frame and picked our way through the darkened room out into the main corridor. As we made our way through the building, I noticed Mason stayed closer and closer to my side. I pulled out my phone and turned on the flashlight.

"Better?" I asked.

"Yeah. Thanks. So, what exactly did you kids get up to in here?"

"Well, just about everything. I had my first kiss in this warehouse."

He stopped and grabbed me around the waist, pulling me in towards him. He took my chin in his hand and tilted my face up, leaning down to kiss me gently. A soft sigh escaped from somewhere within, and he deepened the kiss until I was positively light-headed. By the time he pulled back, I'd completely forgotten where we were.

"Sorry," he said. "Figured I should erase the memory of that first kiss."

"Well done," I said, clearing my throat.

He dropped both hands to my waist, sliding the tips of his fingers up underneath my top. The feel of him against my bare skin was akin to fire licking at my veins. I bit my lip to avoid moaning, suddenly brutally aware of just how much I'd missed him.

He kissed my forehead and when I closed my eyes in pleasure, he kissed my eyelids. I wound my arms around his neck, tilting my head up for another kiss, but he just continued on his merry way, making a trail down along my jawline, his tongue finding the hollow in my neck.

"Ever have sex here?" he murmured.

"No," I sighed. "And that's exactly what I was hoping to rectify today. Before it's too late."

He looked up at me, quizzical.

"Too late?" he asked.

"Yeah. You didn't notice the Sold sign out front?"

"Hmm," he said, looking around. "We're going to get dirty, you know."

"So we'll have a shower."

He ripped off my shirt and bent his head towards my chest. His hands found their way around my back, working the clasp on my bra and letting my breasts fall free. A trembling breath escaped his lips as he cupped my left breast, dipping his head to take my nipple in his mouth. At this point, there was no holding back any noises.

"Oh, God, Mason. I've missed you so much."

His other hand found my right breast and he took my nipple between his thumb and forefinger, rolling back and forth with exquisite pressure. I tugged frantically at his shirt and he pulled away momentarily to pull it over his head in that incredibly sexy way guys had. I ran my hands over his chest, feeling the sparks in my fingertips and the dampness between my legs.

"I've missed you, too," he said, working the zipper on my jeans as I kicked off my shoes. We couldn't get our clothes off fast enough.

He lifted me up onto an old, dusty wooden workbench and dropped to the ground before me. With one hand on each of my knees, he spread my thighs far apart as he leaned in for a first taste. I cried out as my head hit the back wall, but not from pain. For the first time, I truly let myself acknowledge how much I had wanted him over the past weeks. I slid down on the bench, grabbing his head and riding his face as I raced towards what I knew would be an explosive orgasm.

How many nights had I laid in bed, hand between my legs, imagining it was him? How many times had I fantasized about having him watch me from across the room as I touched myself, calling out his name, begging him to come take me. As my body tensed he wrapped his lips around my clit, flicking lightly with his tongue and then sucking in the way he knew drove me over the edge. I screamed as the waves tore through me, wrapping my legs around his neck and pleading with him not to stop.

He slid his hands under my ass, raising my hips off the bench as he continued to devour me from the inside out. The second orgasm came quickly on the heels of the first, causing me to cry out again as he growled deep down in his chest. He pulled away and stood up, pulling me off the bench and turning me to face the wall.

"Fuck, Katie. You're killing me."

He reached for his jeans to find a condom, but I pushed his hand away and reversed our positions, so he was the one up against the wall. I ran my hands down his sides, falling to my knees as I cupped his balls and took his cock in my hand.

"Katie—"

I leaned forward and took him in my mouth, glancing up at him through my lashes to make sure he was watching. He was, hands by his side, grasping the wall for support. I felt him swell in my mouth as I took one hand from the wall and placed it on the back of my head.

"Fuck," he cried.

He slowly started pushing my head back and forth until he was fucking my mouth. I reached down between my legs and slid two fingers inside, so turned on I was unable to stop myself. As I felt him start to constrict, I gave him one last, slow, lazy swipe of my tongue before getting to my feet and gently taking the condom from his hand. I tore off the foil and slid it on all before he could even catch his breath. Then he leaned in, kissed me, and hoisted me up around his waist. He turned and pressed me against the wall before sliding into me. I kept my legs wrapped around him, letting him control the rhythm.

We stared into each other's eyes, silent, as we moved together against the wall. Finally, he began to increase his speed, unable to hold out any longer.

"Katie," he groaned as he came. "Fuck. I love you."

I dropped my legs to the ground as he collapsed against me, head resting on my shoulder as he tried to regain his breath. I reached up and stroked his hair, kissing his neck before whispering in his ear.

"I love you, too."

CHAPTER THIRTY-THREE

A little while later, we were dressed and outside in the back field, lying on our backs in the grass as we watched the sunrise.

"This is breathtaking," Mason said.

"Isn't it?"

"I mean, we have some spectacular scenery in California, but there's something so different about this. It's so pure. Pristine. Those mountains."

I said nothing, letting him bask in the magic of Mountain Valley. After a few moments, I decided it was time to spill the beans.

"I'm making Grace Atkinson's wedding cake."

He turned to me and smiled.

251

"I know. And quite a few others as well. Jessica is very pleased with herself."

I laughed.

"What's going on? There are tons of celebrity bakers. I'm a nobody from Bumblefuck, Canada. Why do they all want me?"

"Because Jessica wanted you. And then they tasted your cake. I told you, Katie. You were made for this. When are you coming out to LA?"

"End of September."

"Stay with me."

I looked at him, shocked.

"For a month?"

"Yes, please. I mean, I'll be shooting and on a crazy schedule, but to know you'll be there, in my house? Please, think about it."

I looked back up at the sky, the fading pinks being slowly replaced by a bright, clear blue. It was going to be another stunner.

"So this place really holds meaning for this town, huh?" he asked, changing the subject.

"Yeah, it really does."

"Think everyone will be mad that I bought it?"

I sat up straight and turned to him, mouth hanging open as I stared in disbelief.

"YOU? Why?"

"Again, I already told you. This town is

252

perfect for a production studio. It's time for me to broaden my horizons, plan for the future when my good looks have faded."

I laughed.

"Never!"

He smiled and leaned over to kiss the top of my head.

"I'm serious. I want to start something here. And you have to admit, it kind of works. You'll be between here and LA, I'll be between here and LA. Imagine if we could coordinate our schedules."

"You're serious?"

"I'm serious."

"You want to be with me?"

"I want to be with you."

I took a deep breath and thought about it for less than a minute.

"But what about all those things you said?"

"I said there had never been anyone worth trying for. Now there is. You've already shown you've got the constitution for it. I've seen clips. You know how to handle the press. And the more well-known you become for your baking, the more you're going to be in the spotlight, anyway." He moved in closer to me, draping an arm across my shoulders. "Let me guide you."

I smiled and looked up at him.

253

"Let's do it together."

He laughed.

"Deal."